The Mystical
Card Reading Handbook

by Lady Deane

The Mystical Card Reading Handbook

Copyright © 2016 by Lady Deane

Cover and Book Design by Molly A Sullivan

International Standard Number
9781934976647

Library of Congress Control Number
2016909756

First Printing 2016

Published by
ACS Publications

an imprint of

Starcrafts LLC
334-A Calef Highway
Epping, New Hampshire 03042

www.astrocom.com
www.starcraftseast.com

Printed in the United States of America

Dedication

For Gram,
the first and best card reader I ever knew.

And for all Seekers of Truth:
May you be granted the Sight
and the Wisdom to know what to do with it.

I originally learned the card system from my grandmother when I was very young. She would often remind me that card reading was not for everyone...that not everyone was meant to know these things. But for those who were, nothing could keep the information from them. The way she explained it, it was as if there were some ancient blessing or mystical spell that provided true seekers with the information sought.

So, for you true seekers out there, here's one more resource for you.
May it find you—and may you find it—illuminating.
Blessed be your quest and the journey you will undertake to achieve it.

An extra special *Thank You* to Jennie and Nell,
who kept me sane, kept me afloat, kept me writing!
Without you two, there would be no book—*friends to the end!*

And a final thank you to Molly Sullivan,
who made my book beautiful.

Table of Contents

♥ ♣ ♦ ♠ ♥ ♣ ♦ ♠

Mary Magdeline Moehringer (Gram)

♥

Introduction
♥ ♣ ♦ ♠ ♥ ♣ ♦ ♠

Walking This Path

There were two people who led me down the metaphysical path—one meant to, one didn't. Still, I learned from them both, and I'd like to think they both would have ended up proud of my accomplishments.

I guess it might surprise some of you to know that most people are not born as tiny baby card readers or astrologers. I had to learn cartomancy and astrology like everyone else. I was, however, born a tiny baby psychic...kind of. I was raised as a psychic by my grandmother, who was a psychic herself, as well as a card reader.

So, I have been doing readings for a very long time. I started when I was about six years old. My grandmother noticed that I seemed to just "know" things, and as she was a psychic reader, she let me do something that she never *ever* let anyone else do—not even her own children or her other grandchildren. She let me watch. I would sit on the floor at the side of her chair; and, as long as I stayed very, very quiet, I could watch her do card readings for the people that came to her. That was pretty magical to me, and that's how I got started.

At first I just observed and listened. Then, after the card reading was finished, Gram would casually ask me what I thought about this or that bit of information that she had given her clients—and that's when the fun started! That is when I got to add my own two cents. At first I thought I was just making up stories. Gram didn't say much at first either, so I didn't know whether she liked my stories or not. But, after awhile she let me know that some of things I had noticed were correct or had come to pass. And, that is when I first learned that the things I saw weren't just my imagination!

Gram had me practice on plants and animals for a few years before she let me do actual card and psychic readings for real live people. I would tell her which plants were thirsty or which animals felt sickly... things like that. In the early days, I mostly read for her many, many cats. She was very fond of cats and was always taking in strays.

Along the way, Gram and I played a lot of fun games together, such as the game of "What's the lady in front of us on the bus thinking?" Or, there was "What does the color Green feel like if you close your eyes and taste it?" game. That one was especially sweet because she used m&ms. (for those of you who may be wondering, green "tastes" like spring and new growing things. I see that color if someone is pregnant).

I didn't know then, that Gram was trying to develop my "sight," as she called it. Through her games, she was teaching me to see without my eyes, to taste without my tongue and to reach out and feel without my hands. Mostly, I just thought I was having fun with my Gram...and who wouldn't want to do that? So, it all developed quite naturally.

My very favorite games of all were the ones we played with the cards—and Gram always had a deck of cards with her. She never left the house without them, so we could play anywhere we traveled. Gram's family was from a small town in Germany, called Emmendingen, in Baden-Würtemberg. As a child, I remember how I loved to play with her beautiful "spielkarten" (playing cards). The German decks seemed so colorful to me with their exotic "Dames" in their fancy dresses (the German Queen card has a "D" on it, meaning Lady), their sporty "Bubes" or "Bauers" (Jacks) and the brave "Konigs" (Kings). From Gram, I learned all about the numbers and the suits.

She also taught me all about the moon (like how you never jar jam during a full moon—because the jars may burst!) However, it wouldn't be until much later that I would learn about how the planets were also involved in the cards.

Neither Gram nor my dad knew anything about astrology. But my dad was a sailor and he did know all about the night sky. He knew all the constellations by name and told me about them when I was about 13. I still remember the first time. It was the 4th of July and Dad, my brother Don and I were lying on our backs on a big blanket up on the roof, just watching the fireworks and eating Ritz crackers (one of Dad's favorites). After awhile the fireworks died down and my little brother fell asleep. We could see the sky very clearly from our perch there on the roof; and after a bit everything went very quiet.

That's when my father just suddenly started pointing out the different constellations as they rose and told me their stories. (If you watch the night sky long enough you'll see several constellations go by). And what stories there were! Gods and Goddesses; Animals and Monsters they all live there in the heavens and they each have a story to tell—and, their stories are our stories and the whole thing just blew me away.

Now, my dad was a man of few words. He wasn't a "gabber," so to speak. So, when he talked like that, I paid close attention. Anyway, that night was a major revelation for me. That's when I first realized that *the heavens are organized, and that the stars have names!* I was beyond amazed. I started studying astrology soon after that. I wanted to know for myself the names of all the planets and the stars—and all of their stories. I've been studying astrology ever since, but I don't know if anyone can ever really know all of their stories. The heavens are vast and they are in constant motion.

Imagine my surprise, when later on, as an adult, I discovered that there was an ancient system of knowledge that combined the meanings of the numbers and the suits in a deck of cards with the stories of the planets! It was a fascinating system and provided a way for me to combine the joint wisdom of my grandmother and my father.

As you might have guessed, I'm still studying the cards. I hope you will too. And, I hope that this handbook of information will inspire you to continue exploring...because none of us can ever know *all* of the stories, but each of us can at least tell our own.

The Cost of Truth

While in the midst of writing this book, I had the most peculiar dream one night. I believe in dreams and in the power of intuition. For some, they represent the mind talking to itself, working things out while we slumber. On the other hand, for those of us who have always heard the voices of angels, well...we know that dreams are often so much more. We go "traveling" at night where we visit the most amazing places and meet the most amazing people. In any case, this particular "dream" (for I'm not at all sure that it was just a dream) was quite vivid, and I remember every detail as though it really happened.

I dreamed that I was wandering in a large and beautiful city. I was tired and thirsty, and I had been walking for hours. I had no money and was worried about how on earth I was going to get home—*and* I was lost. Just then it started to rain, and a thick, menacing fog surrounded me.

As I wandered on, I suddenly and quite inexplicably found myself in front of a large old university. It literally loomed up out of the fog and stopped me in my tracks. The majesty of it took my breath away. It was sort of "Ivy League meets Hogwarts," if you know what I mean (and how could you, really). It was all ancient brick and wood, very impressive in a slightly intimidating yet awe-inspiring, dreamscape kind of way. I walked into the entrance of the first building and directly into what appeared to be a large hall (which I later realized was a mere anteroom to a much larger library). It was filled with magnificent bookshelves from floor to ceiling, all jam packed with lots and lots of books. The whole place was built with highly polished wood and marble...very old, yet very "upper crusty" at the same time.

Suddenly, to my surprise and delight, I came face to face with a large sign with giant pictures of playing cards on it. I peeked around the giant sign. There, behind the sign, and laid out like a feast, were long tables filled to overflowing with every possible poster, deck of cards, and book on card reading that one could possibly imagine! Each one was more fascinating than the last. Every book that I knew of, plus plenty I had never even heard of, were just spread out before me, like some massive book banquet. I couldn't believe my eyes! How incredibly lucky to stumble upon such a treasure trove?

At first, I assumed that this must be some sort of secret "by-invitation-only" type of international seminar on the card system (some of the books were not in English), but as I looked around to ask someone I realized for the first time that I was alone. I looked up at the gigantic clock on the wall—it was exactly noon. It suddenly occurred to me that everyone must have gone out for lunch somewhere.

But what absurdly fantastic luck! Even with no money to pay for the seminar, I would still have at least a half hour before the others returned! If my luck held I would be able to peruse the books and other things completely undisturbed. And so, I gleefully dove in, exploring, reading, touching it all and marveling at the wealth of information that was, quite literally, at my fingertips.

For quite awhile I was completely lost in thought, trying to devour as much as I could in the time that I had, not wanting to waste a precious second. Then, suddenly, I heard a small laugh...like the tinkling of little bells.

I looked up—and then down—and saw what I thought at first to be a child, but then realized was a very tiny woman. She was perfectly proportioned, but was only about three feet tall. But the strangest thing of all was that *she was dressed from head to toe completely in green!* Her eyes were green! Her hair was green and tucked neatly into what appeared to be a green rolled-up leaf made into a smart-looking hat! Her dress was exquisite and made entirely of leaves—small ones at the neck moving into larger more drapey leaves at the bottom—all in a dozen different shades of green. Even her tiny elf-like shoes were green leaves! There was grass green, yellow-green, peapod-green, blue-green, kelly-green, olive-green, forest-green—she was a living, breathing verdant painting! Really, the effect was quite astonishingly beautiful and it brought me up quick.

"Hello," she said, in a high but beautiful melodious voice.

"Oh!" I said (quite surprised that she could speak), "Um, hello."

The tiny Green Lady smiled and appeared to be very friendly, so I smiled back. She took that as an invitation to speak again...and as fate would have it, she appeared to be an expert on the card system! In fact, soon I realized that she had learned a great deal about the cards, as she began pointing out this book and that author and what was especially important about each one. As it turned out, she and I shared some favorite authors; and so we began to converse excitedly about what our individual experiences with card reading had taught us. She was a delightful, intelligent, and most witty conversationalist, and I was quite enjoying our talk.

Then suddenly, from across the room, I heard someone else (perhaps not as friendly as my green companion) clear her throat. I turned around and saw a rather severe and officious-looking woman staring at us. I was so involved in my conversation with the small green one that I hadn't noticed the time...or that someone else had come in!

The disapproving woman looked over at us, eying us quite suspiciously. I looked down and guiltily realized I was still holding some of the books and cards I had been exploring, so I quickly replaced them on the table in their proper places.

I looked sheepishly at the tiny Green Lady and just shrugged and said in a small voice, "Well, I guess it's time for me to go now. I don't belong here and the others will probably be coming back soon. It was nice meeting you, though."

I shook her tiny hand.

I turned then to leave, but the green lady stopped me and laughed that tinkling bell laugh and said. "Why don't be silly! Of *course,* you aren't leaving yet! The very idea!"

Then she really laughed, but there wasn't a drop of malicious intent in it. Her laugh was so easy, so warm and genuine, that I very much wanted to laugh right along with her.

"No, really," I said, when at last we stopped laughing. "This has been fun, and I do wish I could stay, but I really do have to go." Whereupon she continued to completely ignore me and began humming a tune to herself, while proceeding to load my arms with books, charts, decks of cards—whatever she could get her tiny hands on. Horrified, I tried quickly replacing them so we wouldn't draw any more undue attention to ourselves. But as soon as I put one thing down, she tossed me three more things and I was forced to either catch them or let them land in a heap at my feet.

I protested as vigorously as I could without raising my voice too much. "Listen here! I know you mean well, but I can't pay for this! We'll get into trouble!"

To which she simply laughed and replied, "This is free, silly."

I rolled my eyes. Clearly, she did not know what she was saying.

"But really" I finally hissed, "The others will be back soon! I have to get out of here! I don't belong!"

I was close to panic now. I briefly wondered if those in charge of this place would put others in jail for fondling the books? Might this place have a deep dark dungeon somewhere for card reading interlopers?

At that, she stopped short and looked directly at me, quizzically, as though reading my mind and realizing the problem for the first time, and simply said: "But there are no others, Deane. This is all for you. All of it!"

And as she spoke she waved her tiny perfect green arms out over every table, book, card and...well...everything.

I was gob-smacked! I somehow knew, from the way she said it, that it was true. In fact, in that moment—even though I didn't even really know who she was—I knew that she would never say anything to me that was untrue—not ever! I knew it as certainly as I knew my own name, and as strange as it seemed, I believed her completely. It was like having a small epiphany.

"All for me?!" I murmured in amazement.

At that moment I looked down and suddenly there was a backpack in my hand. The tiny green one and I exchanged a brief glance and then smiled hugely at one another because we both had the same exact thought at the same exact same time. Without another word, we proceeded to fill the backpack with everything it could possibly hold (and this must have been a magic backpack, too, because it held an unbelievable amount!).

Then she and I moved to a door at the back of the hall, which led to the largest and most magnificent library I have ever seen. We opened the door, but just as I was about to cross over the threshold, I hesitated and then stopped.

I turned around. Then I summond my courage, squared my shoulders, and stood up very straight. I looked back at the disapproving woman—hard. I looked her directly in the eye, without flinching, as though I were daring her to stop me.

At first she looked quite surprised, then just a tad uncomfortable. And then—the most amazing thing of all happened—she simply lowered her gaze, cleared her throat somewhat sheepishly, and sat down. Then she looked away, as though we had never even been there at all.

I suddenly felt not only as though I were welcome in this library, but as though I belonged there...as only someone "to the manner born" must feel. With the utmost confidence, I stepped though the door to the great library beyond with the absolute conviction that all I had ever wanted to know was in there. Every question I had ever had was about to be answered, and no one and nothing was going to stop me from finding the truth.

The knowledge was mine. The truth was my birthright.
Better still, *I had all the time in the world.*

Truth is Free!
and it will set you free

How to Use This Manual
♥ ♣ ♦ ♠ ♥ ♣ ♦ ♠

Our ordinary deck of playing cards is far from ordinary, and that is by design. The cards represent a microcosm of our universe, and mark our yearly progress in life. Consider our calendar, for example: there are a total of 12 court cards (4 Jacks, 4 Queens, 4 Kings) which stand in for the 12 months of the year (and some say the 12 signs of the zodiac as well); there are 52 cards in the deck which represent the 52 weeks of our year; and there are 4 suits which represent the four seasons.

If you consider the cards by numerological value–where Aces are 1 point each, Twos are 2 points each and so on, up to the Tens (10 points each)–then we begin to see that our days are indeed numbered. When added together, the total value of these is: 220. To that we must also add in the value of the court cards: Jacks are 11 points, Queens are 12 points, and Kings are 13 points. That comes to 144. 220 plus 144 equals 364 days. One Joker is added in to bring the total to 365 days in the average year. There is even a second Joker, to stand in for the extra day in leap years.

Beyond the more obvious correspondences, there are also many metaphysical and hidden correspondences in the cards. The cards, in the right hands, can provide a gateway for an in-depth understanding of ourselves and our place within the cosmos. This is where this humble little manual can be of real value.

In *The Cards Section,* you will find the meanings of every card in every suit under each planetary energy. If you will use this section while you are learning to read cards, you will soon find that the meanings come to you more and more quickly–and before you know it, you will be reading cards like you've done it all your life. And, if you are lucky enough to have been blessed with the wisdom of the Ace of Spades (the true seeker), you will soon discover that the cards have a great deal to say.

Did you know, for instance, that the symbol for the Spades suit represents an inverted leaf from the Tree of Knowledge? Welcome to the mysterious and wonderful world of playing cards!

Terminology

Cartomancy, Cardology, Card Reading...these are all terms used to describe the art of seeing the truth hidden within a standard deck of cards.

My grandmother was the best card reader I have ever met (then or now) and she knew the meanings of all the cards; but she was a psychic long before she ever became a card reader. So, do you have to be psychic to read the cards? No, not at all, but you will find that the very act of reading the cards will develop and enhance your intuition and you should be prepared for this. You also don't have to be an astrologer or numerologist, but knowing a few keywords may help.

Before I studied astrology, I used my grandmother's method of card reading exclusively. However, after learning about the planets, I soon realized that their energies could easily be combined with the card meanings and included in my readings.

Then, as often happens when the student is ready, I found several wonderful old books describing a system of card reading that had already combined the numbers, the card suits, and the planets! Books by Olney Richmond, Florence Campbell, Edith L. Randall, and Arne Lein, to name just a few; and later I found more recent books by Iain McLaren-Owens, Robert Camp, and Thomas Morrell.

It seems that each of the people who helped further the knowledge of the card system, ended up naming it something different. For instance, Olney Richmond called his version the "Mystic Test Book" and believed that the original information came from the Atlantean civilization and represented ancient knowledge. Edith Randall simply called the information "Illumination" and referred to the cards as "Sacred Symbols." Arne Lein said it was "the merging of astrology, numerology and metaphysics" and called it "Metasymbology."

Robert Camp calls it "Destiny Cards;" Iain McLaren-Owens calls it "Astro-Cards;" and Thomas Morrell calls it: the "Time System of Symbolic Astrology." And there are more out that I haven't mentioned!

What these people all have in common is that they have each provided seekers with some wonderful resources that would enrich anyone's card reading experience (see the **Recommended Reading Section**). Do read them. Just know that all these fancy card names, with a few minor differences, mean simply "the study of the cards."

So, please do not let the terminology confuse you, or get in the way of understanding the meanings of the cards. Above all, don't be afraid of learning a few new skills. There are many names for this particular brand of knowledge and there are multiple metaphysical disciplines contained within them. Whatever you choose to call it, card reading has been around a very long time–from purely intuitive readers to the more formal "system" readers and everything in between. And, as long as there are seekers out there who are willing to learn the truth, so it will continue.

The Role of Intuition in Card Reading

The main purpose of this book is to assist card readers with interpreting their readings, and building their skills. This is because, regardless of which reading you are doing or whose techniques you are following, you will find that the meanings of the cards are darn near universal. This discovery was something that truly amazed me in the beginning.

After all, my grandmother never read a single book on card reading. She said that the meanings of the cards just "came" to her one day when she was a young girl playing card games. The meanings she taught me were very close to the meanings that many other authors of books on the card system wrote about (which I discovered years later, when I read them!). But how could my grandmother know about something that she had never studied?

For her, it was simply intuition; she opened herself to the universal language of the cards. To me, this meant that the cards themselves possess a type of divine energy that transcends our current understanding about the way in which we learn things. There is a collective unconscious, and within it lies a vast amount of universal knowledge. I believe that was what my grandmother tapped into, and it has taught me never to underestimate the power of intuition.

Put another way: consider that many years ago astrology and astronomy used to be one wholistic discipline. They each lost something when they were separated. Astronomers today have no idea how much the planets affect human behavior; and many astrologers have no idea what the night sky really looks like! Perhaps it is the same with card information. To the *intellectual* understanding of the card system, we must now add back in the **intuitive** understanding. They must work together.

Of course, having been raised a psychic by my grandmother, perhaps I had a head-start in this department! But after teaching card reading for years, I have witnessed first-hand the development of intuition in people who had previously claimed: "But I don't have a psychic bone in my body!" So just be aware that enhanced intuition is simply a natural side-effect of card reading.

Beginners should also be aware that there are many varied card reading groups out there. Some are quite wonderful, but some try to separate out "psychic" card readings from "other" types of card readings (and these are the ones who often "poo-poo" psychic information as having nothing to do with the card system). They are wrong. Some will even claim that they know the only "right" way to read the cards or interpret the system. Some even call it a science. Don't you fall for it! You will find, when doing readings yourself, that one's destiny is often a changeable and tricky thing to accurately pinpoint. And if everything were already pre-destined, what would be the point of reading the cards at all?

The truth is that reading is far more intricate than one might imagine. Synastry is involved and the result is often a great deal more complex than simply tallying the sum of its parts. And as any experienced card reader can tell you, while learning the meanings of the cards might be considered a by-the-book exercise, the interpretation of the reading as a whole is more of an art. The best readers will combine the power of the intellect *with* the power of the spirit.

When I read for someone, I see the numbers, the suits, and the planets combine into a living, breathing language. And the cards talk to one another! As you might imagine, this special language is not always an easy one to interpret, and that is where your intuition will help you immeasurably.

Also, I have found that there exists a weird sort of pecking order in what I call metaphysical or new age groups. It seems that while scientists may tend to look down upon astrologers and readers, astrologers and card readers tend to look down upon psychics!

Being an astrologer, a card reader *and* a psychic has given me a unique perspective at times. Personally, I think that if everyone just stopped trying so hard for outside validation or legitimacy, we'd all be a lot better off. Inclusion, not exclusion, should be the order of the day.

And that, fellow seekers of true knowledge and wisdom, is my 2 cents on the matter. So, don't let anyone or anything put you off your path. If one group won't accept you, try another, then another. And if none of them will accept you, start your own!

Studying More Advanced Methods

As you begin studying the cards, you will soon realize that this is a vast subject indeed, one that certainly has its more advanced side, but you can start simply. Everyone had to begin somewhere, after all. Also, not everyone was as fortunate as I was to have had a card reading expert in the family! So, start by doing simple readings and build from there. You can do it!

Then, when you are ready for something a bit more challenging, you might try a Solar Return Card Reading. This reading is based on numerology, astrology, and timed quadration techniques, and will require additional resources that contain yearly tables that you can reference.

A few books that contain such tables include:
Sacred Symbols of the Ancients, by Florence Campbell and Edith Randall
Spreads Sets and Card Titles, by Iain Mclaren-Owens
Destiny Cards by Robert Camp

Remember, that even with the more advanced Solar Return Card Reading, you can still use *The Card Interpretation* Section of this handbook to look up the meanings of each card and suit under every planetary energy. Because the main purpose of this book is to assist the card reader with interpreting their reading, regardless of which type of reading is being done, or whose techniques are followed.

Your Birth Card

♥ ♣ ♦ ♠ ♥ ♣ ♦ ♠

Your birth date provides you with an astrological Sun Sign, but did you know that it also provides you with a card? That's right! ONE SINGLE CARD belongs to you. Each and every one of us has one very special card that represents our core personality and divine purpose. That card is called your "Birth Card." Knowing your Birth Card and those of others in your is helpful. When it shows up in a reading, your Birth Card may indicate a period of time of where you are focusing on your own personal goals. The Birth Cards of your friends or family may signify a time when you have more contact with them.

The assignment of birthdays to specific cards comes from an age-old quadration method combined with astrology and numerology. If you'd like to read more about that method begin with Richmond's *Mystic Test Book* (*Resources Section*).

Here are the birthdays associated with each card, presented in two formats. In the first format you can look up a specific card to see which birthdays are associated with it (useful for astrologers or card researchers); in the second format you can look up your own or someone else's birthday to see which Birth Card belongs to them. Both formats contain the exact same information, they are simply organized in different ways.

Once you have identified your birth card, you can read about it in *The Cards Section* under the *Birth Card* explanation for each card (for birth card meanings you may ignore the planetary designations). You might also want to check out the general meaning for each card at the beginning of each new card section, and for more in-depth meanings please see the *Resources Section* for other books on Birth Card meanings.

Cards and Their Birthdays

♥ ♣ ♦ ♠ ♥ ♣ ♦ ♠

Joker   Dec 31 (this is the only birthday for the Joker)

A♥   Dec 30 (this is the only birthday for A♥)

A♣   May 31, Jun 29, Jul 27, Aug 25, Sept 23, Oct 21, Nov 19, Dec 17

A♦   Jan 26, Feb 24, Mar 22, Apr 20, May 18, Jun 16, Jul 14, Aug 12, Sept 10, Oct 8, Nov 6, Dec 4

A♠   Jan 13, Feb 11, Mar 9, Apr 7, May 5, Jun 3, Jul 1

2 ♥   Dec 29 (this is the only birthday for the birthday for the 2♥)

2 ♣   May 30, Jun 28, Jul 26, Aug 24, Sept 22, Oct 20, Nov 18, Dec 16

2 ♦   Jan 25, Feb 23, Mar 21, Apr 19, May 17, Jun 15, Jul 13, Aug 11, Sept 9, Oct 7, Nov 5, Dec 3

2 ♠   Jan 12, Feb 10, Mar 8, Apr 6, May 4, Jun 2

3 ♥   Nov 30, Dec 28

3 ♣   May 29, Jun 27, Jul 25, Aug 23, Sept 21, Oct 19, Nov 17, Dec 15

3 ♦   Jan 24, Feb 22, Mar 20, Apr 18, May 16, Jun 14, Jul 12, Aug 10, Sept 8, Oct 6, Nov 4, Dec 2

3 ♠   Jan 11, Feb 9, Mar 7, Apr 5, May 3, Jun 1

4 ♥   Oct 31, Nov 29, Dec 27

4 ♣   Apr 30, May 28, Jun 26, Jul 24, Aug 22, Sept 20, Oct 18, Nov 16, Dec 14

4 ♦   Jan 23, Feb 21, Mar 19, Apr 17, May 15, Jun 13, Jul 11, Aug 9, Sept 7, Oct 5, Nov 3, Dec 1

4 ♠   Jan 10, Feb 8, Mar 6, Apr 4, May 2

5 ♥   Oct 30, Nov 28, Dec 26

5 ♣   Mar 31, Apr 29, May 27, Jun 25, Jul 23, Aug 21, Sept 19, Oct 17, Nov 15, Dec 13

5 ♦	Jan 22, Feb 20, Mar 18, Apr 16, May 14, Jun 12, Jul 10, Aug 8, Sept 6, Oct 4, Nov 2
5 ♠	Jan 9, Feb 7, Mar 5, Apr 3, May 1
6 ♥	Oct 29, Nov 27, Dec 25
6 ♣	Mar 30, Apr 28, May 26, Jun 24, Jul 22, Aug 20, Sept 18, Oct 16, Nov 14, Dec 12
6 ♦	Jan 21, Feb 19, Mar 17, Apr 15, May 13, Jun 11, Jul 9, Aug 7, Sept 5, Oct 3, Nov 1
6 ♠	Jan 8, Feb 6, Mar 4, Apr 2
7 ♥	Sept 30, Oct 28, Nov 26, Dec 24
7 ♣	Mar 29, Apr 27, May 25, Jun 23, Jul 21, Aug 19, Sept 17, Oct 15, Nov 13, Dec 11
7 ♦	Jan 20, Feb 18, Mar 16, Apr 14, May 12, Jun 10, Jul 8, Aug 6, Sept 4, Oct 2
7 ♠	Jan 7, Feb 5, Mar 3, Apr 1 (April Fool's Day!)
8 ♥	Aug 31, Sept 29, Oct 27, Nov 25, Dec 23
8 ♣	Mar 28, Apr 26, May 24, Jun 22, Jul 20, Aug 18, Sept 16, Oct 14, Nov 12, Dec 10
8 ♦	Jan 19, Feb 17, Mar 15, Apr 13, May 11, Jun 9, Jul 7, Aug 5, Sept3, Oct 1
8 ♠	Jan 6, Feb 4, Mar 2
9 ♥	Aug 30, Sept 28, Oct 26, Nov 24, Dec 22
9 ♣	Jan 31, Feb 29, Mar 27, Apr 25, May 23, Jun 21, Jul 19, Aug 17, Sept 15, Oct 13, Nov 11, Dec 9
9 ♦	Jan 18, Feb 16, Mar 14, Apr 12, May 10, Jun 8, Jul 6, Aug 4, Sept 2
9 ♠	Jan 5, Feb 3, Mar 1
10 ♥	Jul 31, Aug 29, Sept 27, Oct 25, Nov 23, Dec 21

10 ♣	Jan 30, Feb 28, Mar 26, Apr 24, May 22, Jun 20, Jul 18, Aug 16, Sept 14, Oct 12, Nov 10, Dec 8
10 ♦	Jan 17, Feb 15, Mar 13, Apr 11, May 9, Jun 7, Jul 5, Aug 3, Sept 1
10 ♠	Jan 4, Feb 2
J ♥	Jul 30, Aug 28, Sept 26, Oct 24, Nov 22, Dec 20
J ♣	Jan 29, Feb 27, Mar 25, Apr 23, May 21, Jun 19, Jul 17, Aug 15, Sept 13, Oct 11, Nov 9, Dec 7
J ♦	Jan 16, Feb 14, Mar 12, Apr 10, May 8, Jun 6, Jul 4, Aug 2
J ♠	Jan 3, Feb 1
Q ♥	Jul 29, Aug 27, Sept 25, Oct 23, Nov 21, Dec 19
Q ♣	Jan 28, Feb 26, Mar 24, Apr 22, May 20, Jun 18, Jul 16, Aug 14, Sept 12, Oct 10, Nov 8, Dec 6
Q ♦	Jan 15, Feb 13, Mar 11, Apr 9, May 7, Jun 5, Jul 3, Aug 1
Q ♠	Jan 2 (this is the only birthday for the Q♠)
K ♥	Jun 30, Jul 28, Aug 26, Sept 24, Oct 22, Nov 20, Dec 18
K ♣	Jan 27, Feb 25, Mar 23, Apr 21, May 19, Jun 17, Jul 15, Aug 13, Sept 11, Oct 9, Nov 7, Dec 5
K ♦	Jan 14, Feb 12, Mar 10, Apr 8, May 6, Jun 4, Jul 2
K ♠	Jan 1 (this is the only birthday for the K♠)

BIRTHDAYS AND THEIR CARDS

JAN	CARD	FEB	CARD	MAR	CARD	APRIL	CARD	MAY	CARD	JUNE	CARD
1	K♠	1	J♠	1	9♠	1	7♠	1	5♠	1	3♠
2	Q♠	2	10♠	2	8♠	2	6♠	2	4♠	2	2♠
3	J♠	3	9♠	3	7♠	3	5♠	3	3♠	3	A♠
4	10♠	4	8♠	4	6♠	4	4♠	4	2♠	4	K♦
5	9♠	5	7♠	5	5♠	5	3♠	5	A♠	5	Q♦
6	8♠	6	6♠	6	4♠	6	2♠	6	K♦	6	J♦
7	7♠	7	5♠	7	3♠	7	A♠	7	Q♦	7	10♦
8	6♠	8	4♠	8	2♠	8	K♦	8	J♦	8	9♦
9	5♠	9	3♠	9	A♠	9	Q♦	9	10♦	9	8♦
10	4♠	10	2♠	10	K♦	10	J♦	10	9♦	10	7♦
11	3♠	11	A♠	11	Q♦	11	10♦	11	8♦	11	6♦
12	2♠	12	K♦	12	J♦	12	9♦	12	7♦	12	5♦
13	A♠	13	Q♦	13	10♦	13	8♦	13	6♦	13	4♦
14	K♦	14	J♦	14	9♦	14	7♦	14	5♦	14	3♦
15	Q♦	15	10♦	15	8♦	15	6♦	15	4♦	15	2♦
16	J♦	16	9♦	16	7♦	16	5♦	16	3♦	16	A♦
17	10♦	17	8♦	17	6♦	17	4♦	17	2♦	17	K♣
18	9♦	18	7♦	18	5♦	18	3♦	18	A♦	18	Q♣
19	8♦	19	6♦	19	4♦	19	2♦	19	K♣	19	J♣
20	7♦	20	5♦	20	3♦	20	A♦	20	Q♣	20	10♣
21	6♦	21	4♦	21	2♦	21	K♣	21	J♣	21	9♣
22	5♦	22	3♦	22	A♦	22	Q♣	22	10♣	22	8♣
23	4♦	23	2♦	23	K♣	23	J♣	23	9♣	23	7♣
24	3♦	24	A♦	24	Q♣	24	10♣	24	8♣	24	6♣
25	2♦	25	K♣	25	J♣	25	9♣	25	7♣	25	5♣
26	A♦	26	Q♣	26	10♣	26	8♣	26	6♣	26	4♣
27	K♣	27	J♣	27	9♣	27	7♣	27	5♣	27	3♣
28	Q♣	28	10♣	28	8♣	28	6♣	28	4♣	28	2♣
29	J♣	29	9♣	29	7♣	29	5♣	29	3♣	29	A♣
30	10♣			30	6♣	30	4♣	30	2♣	30	K♥
31	9♣			31	5♣			31	A♣		

JULY	CARD	AUG	CARD	SEPT	CARD	OCT	CARD	NOV	CARD	DEC	CARD
1	A♠	1	Q♦	1	10♦	1	8♦	1	6♦	1	4♦
2	K♦	2	J♦	2	9♦	2	7♦	2	5♦	2	3♦
3	Q♦	3	10♦	3	8♦	3	6♦	3	4♦	3	2♦
4	J♦	4	9♦	4	7♦	4	5♦	4	3♦	4	A♦
5	10♦	5	8♦	5	6♦	5	4♦	5	2♦	5	K♣
6	9♦	6	7♦	6	5♦	6	3♦	6	A♦	6	Q♣
7	8♦	7	6♦	7	4♦	7	2♦	7	K♣	7	J♣
8	7♦	8	5♦	8	3♦	8	A♦	8	Q♣	8	10♣
9	6♦	9	4♦	9	2♦	9	K♣	9	J♣	9	9♣
10	5♦	10	3♦	10	A♦	10	Q♣	10	10♣	10	8♣
11	4♦	11	2♦	11	K♣	11	J♣	11	9♣	11	7♣
12	3♦	12	A♦	12	Q♣	12	10♣	12	8♣	12	6♣
13	2♦	13	K♣	13	J♣	13	9♣	13	7♣	13	5♣
14	A♦	14	Q♣	14	10♣	14	8♣	14	6♣	14	4♣
15	K♣	15	J♣	15	9♣	15	7♣	15	5♣	15	3♣
16	Q♣	16	10♣	16	8♣	16	6♣	16	4♣	16	2♣
17	J♣	17	9♣	17	7♣	17	5♣	17	3♣	17	A♣
18	10♣	18	8♣	18	6♣	18	4♣	18	2♣	18	K♥
19	9♣	19	7♣	19	5♣	19	3♣	19	A♣	19	Q♥
20	8♣	20	6♣	20	4♣	20	2♣	20	K♥	20	J♥
21	7♣	21	5♣	21	3♣	21	A♣	21	Q♥	21	10♥
22	6♣	22	4♣	22	2♣	22	K♥	22	J♥	22	9♥
23	5♣	23	3♣	23	A♣	23	Q♥	23	10♥	23	8♥
24	4♣	24	2♣	24	K♥	24	J♥	24	9♥	24	7♥
25	3♣	25	A♣	25	Q♥	25	10♥	25	8♥	25	6♥
26	2♣	26	K♥	26	J♥	26	9♥	26	7♥	26	5♥
27	A♣	27	Q♥	27	10♥	27	8♥	27	6♥	27	4♥
28	K♥	28	J♥	28	9♥	28	7♥	28	5♥	28	3♥
29	Q♥	29	10♥	29	8♥	29	6♥	29	4♥	29	2♥
30	J♥	30	9♥	30	7♥	30	5♥	30	3♥	30	A♥
31	10♥	31	8♥			31	4♥			31	Joker

Curiosities

Many card students have asked why some cards represent many birth dates, while others represent only one or only a few. The card formula is based on quadration, numerology and astrology (see Olney Richmond's *Mystic Test Book* in the Resources Section). However, I like to imagine that this is a little bit like people's astrological or Sun Signs. They are not evenly divided either. The number of Aries Sun Sign people born into the world, for instance, is not equal to the number of Virgo Sun Sign people born.

Although, interestingly, one study on zodiac signs and birth frequency did seem to indicate that Aquarius was the least populated Sun Sign—meaning that there tend to be fewer births occurring between Jan 20th and Feb 14th of any year. Do cooler temperatures have something to do with birth frequency? Your guess is as good as mine.

And do you know what? Other people have wondered about birth frequency too. The New York Times actually did a study of US births between 1973 and 1999 and discovered that September 16th was the most popular birthday of the year (Go Virgo! and/or the 8♣).

At least during that particular time period. In 2006 for example, August was the most popular month for births. And late summer and early fall—in August and September—were the months with the most births overall.

The individual days with the least number of births were New Year's Day, Christmas Day, and Feb 29th. Of course, that might have more to do with doctors being less willing to give up their holidays and golf dates to deliver babies! And also, of course, leap year. But overall, the early fall was the most popular time for birthdays. Why is this? Do we, as a species, tend to mate within some sort of predetermined pattern? I do not know the answer to this, but it would make a fascinating study!

Meanwhile, if you'd like to know more about the New York Times study, please visit their website:

nytimes.com/2006/12/19/business/20leonhardt-table.html.

To Read or Not to Read
♥ ♣ ♦ ♠ ♥ ♣ ♦ ♠

Getting Started

If you are new to card reading—or just new to reading with a standard deck of 52 cards (as opposed to tarot cards or some other system of card divination)—then may I suggest you begin simply. Perhaps you could do a regular reading for yourself, once each week.

A weekly reading is an invaluable tool, even for advanced card readers. This is because the better you become at reading for yourself, the more you are likely to be able to see for others. There are 52 weeks in one year, so if you commit to doing one reading a week for an entire year, that would be 52 chances to develop in depth knowledge of the cards. And it allows you to become intimately acquainted with your own personal deck of cards. This is important, because the more you use your deck, the more it will respond to your individual energy.

For all you beginning card students out there, I will suggest—just for your first year—that you only read for yourself, your family or your close friends (in other words, people who are likely to forgive your "beginner" mistakes).

May I also suggest that you do not charge them a fee for the reading. It is an old (and wise) custom for true seekers to donate a one-year period of apprenticeship to the universe. During that time, all readings are offered up as a gift to the divine source of all knowledge and inspiration. In return, you ask that the universe bless your efforts by increasing your skill with the cards and enhancing your psychic gifts. Believe me when I say, that the time will pass quickly, your knowledge and skills will develop rapidly, and the whole experience will have been well worth it.

Choosing Your Cards

As long as your deck contains 52 cards (plus Jokers, if you use them), you may select any deck you like as your personal deck (please see the *Jokers* page in *The Cards Section* pertaining to the optional use of the Jokers). There is no one "official" deck of cards used for divination purposes that I know of. Some, of course, are made in the timeless design such as the Bicycle®, "Bee"®, Hoyle®, Aviator® and Tally-Ho® brand playing cards, to name just a few. In addition to the timeless classics, there are also many wonderful artistic or specialty card decks (please see *The Resources Section* at the end of this manual for some suggestions to get you started). My grandmother taught me that any deck of cards that decorates the Ace of Spades (which is most of them) is acceptable.

If you've never noticed it before, now's the time to take out your deck and check out the Ace of Spades. Most decks will give a special little "flourish" to this one Ace. Manufacturers will often choose to put their logo here. The Ace of Spades rules the deck and the ancient art of Cartomancy and divination, so it is treated with a bit of extra respect. I once found a deck that I really liked. It was a very artistic and unique deck, but they had chosen not to decorate their Ace of Spades. So I did (Gram would have been so proud!). Keep your trusty Sharpie marker—black, of course—always at the ready.

Did you know that the cards did not originally have numbers on them? They were just symbols. Hearts, Clubs, Diamonds, and Spades are common today in America, but in Germany they were Hearts, Acorns, Bells, and Leaves. These symbols were called "pips," or sometimes just spots. You can still find reproductions of these "pip only" decks today, although most card decks now include both pips and numbers for easy identification. Either type is acceptable for divination. In some of the more artistic decks, the pips may be changed, or redesigned in some way, to fit the theme of the art deck. Some of them are quite imaginative, too (like the sausage pips in the Bacon deck!). However, this should not affect the way in which you use the deck.

While finding your own personal favorite card deck may be something of a scavenger hunt, finding an ordinary standard card deck could not be easier. Literally. They are in every convenience, grocery, or dollar store around. Every airport I have ever been in has sold their own deck of cards....usually with pictures of their state or city on them. Also, the price of a deck has not really gone up much over the years. You can still get a brand new deck for about six bucks or less; and if you shop the thrift stores or yard sales you may find them for as little as a quarter. Although, in this case (especially if the deck is unsealed), you should count the cards to make sure there are 52. For used cards, you might also want to cleanse them (please see the section on *Cleansing Your Cards*).

I speak from experience here. I once bought an open deck and when I got home I found that the Aces were missing. Not to be deterred, I cut up some card stock to the right size and drew in my own Aces (and yes, I gave an extra little "flourish" to the Ace of Spades!).

Nowadays, I maintain at least two working decks for myself to use for my own weekly readings, and an entire large bowl of different card decks for visitors and clients. Seriously, it's like a giant candy bowl, except it's full of cards!

If my clients come for an in-person reading, I allow them to pick their own deck from the bowl. For phone readings I select a deck at random to read with (although we all know that there's nothing random about it!). As you might imagine, when you read cards for a living you are often presented with interesting decks of cards as gifts, and that is how I managed to collect my "bowl of cards."

Sometimes card students ask me what the difference is between the various types of card decks. Here is a breakdown of some of the decks you may come across in your search:

Standard Deck of 52

This is 52 cards, Ace through King, 13 cards per suit, 4 suits (plus 2 optional Jokers), 2 colors (by the way, Jokers were an American addition to the deck). Standard cards usually measure 2.5 inches wide by 3.5 inches tall. This is usually my first choice for Cartomancy.

Poker Deck

This is pretty much exactly like the standard deck. In fact, most Poker decks are called "Standard Poker" deck. They are the same size and have all of the same features as the Standard deck. Who knows, perhaps casinos just like their cards to say "Poker" on them. A Poker deck can certainly be used for Cartomancy.

Bridge Deck

This deck has the same number and type of cards as the standard deck, but is slightly narrower. Bridge Cards measure 2.25 inches wide by 3.5 inches tall. Bridge players often have to hold many more cards than Poker players do, so the narrower width is helpful (Whist is an English game similar to Bridge). I don't personally use these cards for Cartomancy, but you could.

Pinochle Deck

This deck has two each of the 9, 10, Jack, Queen, King and Ace card in each of the 4 suits, 48 cards per deck. The Pinochle deck has no Jokers. I used to think that the Pinochle deck was not really suitable for Cartomancy. But I have to be honest here, and admit that on a few occasions I did see my grandmother use a Pinochle deck to give readings when a regular standard deck was unavailable. And do you know what? She made it work.

Canasta Deck

Canasta actually uses a double deck. It's played by combining 2 full sets of 54 cards (both Jokers are used) for a total of 108 cards. The game of Canasta has a unique and somewhat complicated scoring system and the Canasta point value of each card is printed on its face. So they are generally not suitable for Cartomancy.

SKAT Deck

This is a German card game which has 32 cards: 4 suits with 8 cards each: Ace, King, Queen, Jack, 10, 9, 8, 7. Some of the German decks have different suits: Hearts (Hearts), Acorns (Clubs), Bells (Diamonds), and Leaves (Spades). The Spades are Green and the Diamonds are Yellow. Can you read with this deck? I can (and have).

JASS Deck

This is a Swiss card game containing 36 cards: 4 suits with 9 cards each: Ace, King, Queen, Jack, 10, 9, 8, 7, 6. This game may have been the forerunner to the American game of Pinochle. My grandmother was particularly fond of Pinochle and I often wondered if this was because she missed her family games of Jass! Could *you* read with this deck?

Doppelkopf Deck

This is an odd German card game which has 48 cards: 4 suits with 6 cards each but doubled (2 decks are used): Ace, 10, King, Queen, Jack, 9. It's played with 4 people and 2 teams, but the team pairs don't know who each other is at the start of the game! So far I have not used this deck for Cartomancy.

Paper or Plastic?

Most standard decks of cards are made in either the "Paper" or "Plastic" variety. Paper decks are actually paper that are plastic-coated, and plastic decks are made from 100% plastic. Paper decks are less slippery than plastic decks and they cost about half as much as the plastic does. Plastic decks cost more, but they are washable, last longer and are a good choice if a deck will see repeated use.

In the end though, I think it just comes down to what feels better. Try both for yourself and see what you like. Even though I use my decks frequently, I do tend to prefer the paper decks. To me, they just feel better in my hand.

Cleansing Your Cards

Cleansing may be needed for a variety of reasons. If you purchase an unsealed or previously used deck, it's probably a good idea to cleanse and purify the energy in the deck before attempting to use it. Also, if you have many clients there will eventually be a build up of energy that should be cleansed every now and again. I have found once a year to be entirely sufficient for cards that see regular use. But occasionally, more often might become necessary.

For instance, if you have ever had a particularly "heavy" reading—the kind that leaves a residue behind in the room after the client has left—then you can imagine how dark the energy on the cards can become. I salt those decks immediately then set them aside for a time of rest. In any case, it's a good idea to periodically rotate your card decks anyway because it provides you with a new start and a fresh perspective.

To Cleanse Your Cards

♠ Wrap your cards (case and all, if your cards came with one) within a handkerchief, dishtowel, piece of muslin, or any clean scrap of fabric you have handy.

♠ Place the wrapped cards in the bottom of a bowl and pour enough salt over the top to completely cover the deck. Regular table salt is fine, or you can use coarse sea salt, if you prefer. All salts have a cleansing quality to them (that is why people use bath salts when they bathe, they draw out the impurities).

♠ Leave the deck overnight to allow time for the cards to release any impurities into the salt. Then, you can discard the salt (but don't dump it outside! It will kill the plants).

♠ Lastly, consecrate the cards to your purpose. Each one of us will likely have our own personal and individual method for this.

To me, part of the consecration process means that I would no longer use that deck for card games (Poker, Spades, Old Maid....it doesn't really matter which games you normally play). A deck used for reading purposes should be consecrated for reading purposes alone and set apart from those decks used regularly for card games.

I am not saying here that readings can't be viewed as entertainment. Many people do enjoy their readings. But experienced cartomancers know that there are also times when the readings become quite serious, and those cards are not meant for games or parlor tricks.

When to Read

Well, first things first, I say, and deciding when to read probably has a much longer and more involved answer. Truthfully, there are many legitimate reasons that people might have for reading for themselves or others. But for now, I'll keep it simple. A reading is done when you want to develop your intuition, to find answers that your other senses may not be able to provide, to seek clarity about a specific situation, to obtain divine guidance, to establish more than just a passing acquaintance with your higher self, to use your gift to help others, and for entertainment.

Yes, believe it or not, there are times when readings are highly entertaining! But readings can and do often give more information than you would expect. So, reader beware! The cards often have the last laugh.

...or Not to Read

And then there are those times when you should definitely NOT do a reading, like when you are tired, ill, angry or just out of sorts. Or, how about when you've been drinking; or when everyone else has been drinking? Say you're at a party and everyone is either drunk or high (yes, in case you're wondering, I learned this one from experience when I was 19 and was hired as the "entertainment" for a New Year's eve party!). So, just spare yourself the grief and do not read then.

Or, how about when you are rushed or don't really have the time required to process the information fully? Don't read then, wait for a better time. Or when you throw a reading that makes no sense (I call this one "bad juju." It gives me the shivers). Or when you are unclear about what you want to know. Or, how about when you are clear about what you want to know, but knowing the answer won't actually help you?

In other words, don't read when you know there is no possibility of changing the outcome, or when you don't really want to know the answer to your question in the first place! Face it, there are just some things in life that we are better off not knowing. Leave them to fate.

Preparation Before Reading

In addition to preparing your cards before a reading, it's also a good idea to prepare yourself, so that you might be open to receive the information that will come through you. This is a quick and painless process and takes only a few moments of your time.

First, center yourself and take a few deep breaths. Then take a moment to focus your energies. Ask for divine guidance so that your reading may show you what you most need to know (and not what you most want to know, which may be two different things).

Then, you can say any prayer you are comfortable with, or you can just simply state your intention. The idea is to create a sacred, protected space into which information can safely pass. I like to think of it as creating a state of "divine grace."

My own prayer is a simple one and goes something like this:

I am a child of Divine Light.
May I be granted the sight,
and the wisdom to know how to use it.
I ask this by the God and Goddess
who within me dwell.

Amen and Blessed Be

Types of Readings

There are about as many types of readings and variations on card layouts as there are people who read cards. We all have our own methods. Here I present you with some basic readings that I have found useful over the past 33 years. You will notice that they progress in complexity, as well as the time or the talent that is required. If you are a beginner, start with one of the first four types listed until you become familiar with the cards and how they work. Practice combining the card energies, as this is the best way to learn. Also, don't forget to write your readings down in a journal or notebook. One learns many things with hindsight, and reviewing your readings is an excellent way to further your knowledge of the cards.

A Simple YES or NO Reading

A Single Question Reading

The Weekly Reading

The General Reading (3-6 months)

The Monthly Reading

The Yearly or Birthday Reading

The Solar Return Card Reading

A Simple Yes or No Reading

When I say "simple" here, I mean it. This reading is only for the simplest possible questions. You pose a question, you randomly pick one card to answer it. These must be the questions that you know ahead of time will be answered by either a "yes" or "no," and usually nothing more. If your question has any kind of complication to it, you are probably better off doing a Single Question Reading.

Your first step is to decide what cards will represent YES and which cards will stand in for NO. For instance, you can use all BLACK cards for YES and all RED cards for NO. Simple, easy, direct. Likewise, you could use all even numbered cards to indicate a YES answer and all odd-numbered cards to mean a NO answer.

Of course you could just allow the deck to choose which cards will stand in for YES and NO. Simply fan out the cards in front of you and focus on YES then ask the deck: "Which card shall be YES for me?" then select a card. Do the same for NO. Whatever method you choose—stick with it. The key to a simple reading is keeping it simple–that and consistency.

Finally, you may wish to select the cards for YES and NO yourself. For instance, I generally use Tens for YES and Nines to mean NO. This is easy to remember because Tens generally mean success and Nines represent completions or endings. If I draw any other card besides a Nine or Ten I would take that to mean "maybe" or "try again later" (which is kind of like the old-time Magic 8-Ball, only with cards!). A card other than a Nine or Ten could also indicate that the matter is more complicated than a simple YES or NO reading might allow. In that case, simply do a more complex reading and see if that clears things up.

A Single Question Reading

Wherein I climb upon my soapbox about "Clarity." You have been warned! Use this reading ONLY when you have one single question that you need clarification on. Some examples of the types of acceptable questions for this reading are (and these are actual questions that clients have asked me over the years):

"Will I get that promotion at work?"
"Will I get fired"
"Will I get paid for the project I just completed?"
"Which job should I accept?"
"Will I get into (XYZ...) college?"
"Should I take a trip now?"
"Is he/she right for me?"
"Will I marry this year?"
"Am I being deceived?"
"Is the illness serious?"
"Will our house sell?"
"Should I relocate?"

When you initially attempt to sit with your question, the most likely thing to happen is that other questions will start popping up as well. For example: "Will he call me?" may quickly be followed up in your mind by "What should I wear on our date?" or "Will his family like me?" or "Will we have sex?" or even "Is he the one?" and on and on.

But when, at last, you arrive at ONE SINGLE QUESTION, it is much more likely to be the only question that stays with you (i.e.: "Will I find love?"). So, you can be certain you've reached clarity when one question, and only one question, remains.

Once you have your question, three cards are used to answer it. I use no more and no less. "Well, why not use just one card?" you may very well ask. Because, I have found that few questions are really *so* simple that one card will cover all the intricacies contained within them (see the YES/NO Reading for further clarification).

In my experience, most questions have many layers to them, some conscious and some not. Three cards allow me to see the actual answer quickly, but also provide me with some important information around the question. I don't throw more than three cards per question, because that usually ends up just morphing into a full-blown reading. Which, of course you can do if need be, but if your intention is to truly ask that "one single question," then three cards should do the job nicely.

Also, the three cards do not need to be read in any specific order. Some like to think of them as representing "past, present, and future," but for me, it's much more important to blend the meanings of all the cards together accurately than to worry about which card stands for what. If your question truly is a simple one, the answer becomes clear and the card positions are less important than the overall message.

Another important point: I don't pay any attention (in any of my readings) to whether or not a card is inverted. In other words, as I throw the cards down, if one happens to land up-side-down, I just turn it right-side-up. Some readers give a different interpretation to an inverted card. I do not.

To throw the cards for a single question, simply sit still until the question clarifies in your mind (or instruct the person for whom you are reading to do so). Most people think that they know what they want to ask, but often in the middle of asking it, they become aware that their real question was something quite different.

For example, I had a client who asked the question: "Will Jack call me?" (not his real name). But as I began to read for her, it became apparent that what she asked and what she really needed to know were two very different things. For her, I threw a Two of Clubs (meaning yes, he will call you for a date), then a Six of Hearts and a Seven of Hearts.

Now, the Six of Hearts is relationship karma and this may have been warning her that Jack was either someone from her past or perhaps a past-life connection. Or, it might have been warning her that after a hopeful start the relationship would stall. Neither of these possibilities would necessarily put the kibosh on their love. However, when followed by the Seven of Hearts, it is not generally favorable news.

The Seven warns her of romantic challenges and when combined with the karmic indicators of the Six it probably meant that this person was there specifically to help her see an unhealthy karmic pattern that she needed to dissolve. The Six was trying to say to her: "Think it over, protect your heart!"

Perhaps she was picking "Mr. Wrong" over and over again because it felt familiar to her (as in a past life pattern), and most likely this would continue to happen until she learned to dissolve the karma thru awareness and right choices. Were this relationship going to work out well, I would have expected to see the Two or Four of Hearts, not the Six and Seven. I know it's an old-fashioned expression, but being at "6s and 7s" literally means to be off-balance, disorganized or befuddled.

So, you can see that while the answer was "yes, he will call" the cards were also trying to tell her that perhaps he was not the one who should be calling. He was not right for her and, in short order they broke up and she was back again asking the question she really wanted to know the answer to in the first place, which was: "Will I find love?"

CLARITY, dear reader, is worth the effort required. Take a moment, breathe deep, think about what you *really* need to know. Then, when the question has truly clarified in your mind, ask it.

For those of you who are uncertain about how to know when you are "clear" about your question here is the sum total of my advice, based on many years of helping people ask the right questions in their readings so as not to waste their time (or mine).

YOU ARE CLEAR ABOUT YOUR QUESTION WHEN THERE ARE NO OTHER QUESTIONS POPPING INTO YOUR HEAD

In *The Art of Interpretation Section* of this handbook, I have included a sample Single Question Reading so you can see how to interpret the cards and blend their energies. When you feel ready to do your own reading, you can look up the meanings of your cards in *The Cards Section*. When reading cards for a Single Question, simply ignore the planetary energies and use the card meanings under "Summary Card."

The Weekly Reading

A weekly reading can be a beginner's best friend. It will help familiarize you with the card system as well as provide you with important information for your upcoming week. Some people feel that reading every week is a bit too much. In that case, you might decide to just read for those weeks that you expect to be particularly eventful. However, let me just say that reading every week will allow you to know the cards in a very personal and immediate way, because the very best way to actually learn Cartomancy is to practice it!

I lay out my weekly reading with nine cards total. Other readers might use more or less for their weekly readings and that is fine, as long as you are consistent about it. I would probably not use less than eight total, however, because you need at least one card for each of the planetary energies: Mercury thru Pluto.

To begin my reading I shuffle the cards, cut them in thirds, throw 8 cards straight in a row, and then throw a 9th card—the final Summary Card—on top, just above the others.

The first eight cards carry the energies of planets in this order:

1st card is Mercury
2nd card is Venus
3rd card is Mars
4th card is Jupiter
5th card is Saturn
6th card is Uranus
7th card is Neptune
8th card is Pluto

You can find keywords for the planets in *The Art of Interpretation Section* of this manual. So, for example, when using some of the more common keywords for the eight cards above:

1st or **Mercury Card** would be filtered through Mercury's energies and would have something to do with the thought process, the mind, communications of all sorts, writing, speaking, emailing, etc.

2nd or **Venus Card** would be filtered through Venus energies such as family, friends, love, relationships, home, or artistic pursuits.

3rd or **Mars Card** would reflect passion, ambition, anger, or physical energy.

4th or **Jupiter Card** would represent expansion, growth, the big picture, education and travel opportunities.

5th or Saturn Card would embody hard work, achievements, employment, career path, work projects or self-discipline.

6th or Uranus Card might show where you will be surprised, where plans, people or ideas may change, or events that might pop up suddenly.

7th or Neptune Card may show psychic or spiritual happenings during the week, or where you may be confused or disillusioned.

8th or Pluto Card can tell you where you may face the greatest challenge during the week or where you may experience a personal transformation of some kind (I call it my personal "ah-ha!" moment).

The last card, the **Summary Card,** ties all the other cards in together and sums up the overall energy or vibration of your week, or shows you an important overriding theme for the week.

In *The Art of Interpretation Section,* I have included two sample weekly readings so you can see how to interpret the cards and blend their energies. When you are ready to do your own Weekly Reading, you can look up the meanings of your cards in *The Cards Section* of this handbook.

The Timing of Your Weekly Reading

The first step for beginning readers to decide is WHEN to do their weekly readings. If you're reading for yourself, then you must choose a day on which to start. Just as your year has a personal starting point (which is your birthday), your week also has a personal starting point. Traditionally, you would do your readings on the day prior to the day of the week on which you were born.

In other words, if you were born on a Sunday, then your weekly reading day would always be Saturday. Your weekly reading starts the day after you read it. So, if you were born on a Sunday, then every Saturday you would set aside some time to do a reading for yourself. This helps you to prepare for your week ahead.

Of course you can begin your weekly reading on any day that is convenient. As long as you are consistent, you should have good results.

The General Reading

A General Reading is good when you need some guidance, but you don't really have one specific question. I have found that when I do a General Reading, the information provided by the reading usually covers a 3-6 month period of time. It can cover a lot of ground and can alert you to whatever issues you need to address in the immediate future. This reading is an excellent choice for people who like to just "check-in" every now and again, but don't really want a regularly scheduled reading. This is also an excellent reading for clients who are not really sure what they want to know. For the General Reading I usually employ the traditional Celtic Cross setup for the cards.

To throw a Celtic Cross, shuffle the cards as you normally would, cut the deck, then lay one card in the middle. This is your main card. Now lay one card across it. Then lay out four cards in a cross pattern around the center 2 cards: one below the main card, one to the left, one above it, and one to the right of it. Lastly, lay out four cards straight up in a line, from bottom to top.

The main card—the one in the center—will tell you a lot about the current situation of the person you are reading for. This is probably what they most have on their minds at the time of the reading, their key issues, so to speak; or it can represent what they most need to know (and this is helpful because they do not always know what it is they most need to know, either, so they aren't likely to ask questions around it).

The card that crosses the main card will say something important that is directly related to the situation described by the main card. It may be a challenge to the central query or it may be a help or blessing.

The card directly to the right of the main card represents the past—but only that part of the past that has some bearing on the current issues. The card directly below the main card represents the present.

The card to the left of the main card refers to the near future (about 1-3 months) and the card directly above the main card refers to the distant future (about 4-6 months).

The 4 cards lying in a straight line act as summary cards and can give additional information about potential outcomes to the current or future situation; while the final card is considered the mostly likely final outcome of events, should the present course not be altered.

The Monthly Reading

A Monthly Reading (which may also be called a Lunar Reading) can be done if you prefer to read for yourself once a month, rather than once a week. As the name implies, this reading is done once a month.

This reading generally follows the lunar cycle. You can choose to read during either the New Moon or the Full Moon. Both times have energies to recommend them, but if you're unsure how to begin, allow me to suggest the New Moon. This is a naturally intuitive time of month. At the New Moon possibilities are still growing and forming and we have the chance to "begin again" in some important way. If we set our intentions at the New Moon, we may see some of them grow and blossom with the Full Moon. Again, consistency is important. Whichever lunar phase you select, try to stick with that cycle for awhile at least, to see how those energies work for you personally.

For the Monthly Reading I generally use five cards—one card to represent each week of the lunar cycle, plus one Summary Card. As with most readings I do, I keep the layout as simple as possible. I layout four cards straight across in a row with the Summary Card on top, one card to represent each week. Then you combine their meanings and blend their energies to see a true picture of your overall month.

Another way to do a Monthly Reading—and this is mainly for astrologers—is to follow your actual lunar return cycle. This requires some knowledge of your natal chart. The astrological lunar return is the time when the Moon in the sky returns to your own personal Moon— the place it held on the day and moment of your birth. In other words, this is when the current transiting Moon Sign (the one in constant motion in the sky above your head) matches the Moon Sign in your natal astrology chart. The Moon changes signs approximately once every 2-3 days, so about once a month it will match or "return" to your own natal Moon by sign and degree.

If you are an astrologer, this is easy to do. Simply calculate your lunar returns for one year (or you can go to astrocom.com and order any lunar return calculations quite easily). Then simply time your reading for the day prior to your lunar return date for each month.

The Yearly or Birthday Reading

The Yearly Reading (my Grandmother called it the Birthday Reading) is done once per year, usually on one's birthday or the day before the birthday. Gram believed that doing the reading on one's actual birthday added a special blessing to your year. This reading covers one year, but it is not the calendar year. It is your personal year and is in effect from your birthday one year until your birthday the next year.

For this reading you deal out 12 cards—one for each month of the year, beginning with your birth month—and one Summary Card, for a total of 13 cards. You can deal them into a circle formation, with the Summary Card at the center, or you can deal them straight out with the Summary Card at the top or at the bottom.

For this reading, the layout is not as important as the number and order of the cards. The 1st Card represents your birth month, the 2nd Card represents the month after your birth, the 3rd card represents the month after that, and so on, until you reach the 12th Card which represents the month just before your next birthday. The 13th Card summarizes the total energy for the year and represents one very important theme which will play out during your year.

A Birthday Reading is not meant to show you everything that will happen during the year. Think of it as a sort of checklist of some of the more important highlights of your year.

The Solar Return Card Reading

The Solar Return Card Reading covers one year, but once again, it is not the calendar year. It is your personal year and is in effect from your birthday one year until your birthday the next year. This is an example of one of the more advanced readings I spoke about in the introduction. It is a different and more complex reading than the more simplified Birthday reading previously described. They both look at your upcoming year, so they have that in common. However, the Solar Return Reading is based upon advanced, timed quadration methods, and will require additional resources with yearly tables for you to refer to.

Examples of books that contain such tables include:

Sacred Symbols of the Ancients, by Florence Campbell & E. Randall
Destiny Cards, by Robert Camp
Spreads Sets and Card Titles, by Iain Mclaren-Owens

For further instructions on how to set up a Solar Return Reading, please refer to books by these authors in the **Recommended Reading Section.**

How you set up your Solar Return Reading depends upon whose method you will be using. For example, in Robert Camp's Destiny Card method, there are 2 cards that represent each of 7 planetary periods: Mercury through Neptune (note: many authors on the card system do not include Pluto in their planetary periods). Each planetary period represents approximately 52 days of your year (52 days x 7 planets = 364 days). If you do use Robert Camp's method, please note that the first card is generally considered the more powerful of the two, although both cards must be combined for the most accurate meaning.

The second card is truly a secondary influence and the primary influence for the period will always be represented by the first card. Also, in some years the Neptune period will have only one card. Robert's method also employs 3 Summary cards for the year: the Long Range Card, the Pluto Card, and the Results Card.

An even more in-depth Solar Return Reading method, by Iain McLaren-Owens, utilizes 3 cards per cycle (13 cycles): one card for the Solar Return, one from the Pure Spread and one from the Life Spread for each of 13 cycles. This would provide 36 cards to interpret for the reading—13 cards for the specific year and then 13 each for the underlying Pure Spread and Life Spread. And Thomas Morell offers yet another in depth version of a solar return card reading. As you will see as you research them, these types of readings are advanced and can take some time to understand how to set up and interpret. They do provide in depth knowledge and offer even more dimension to card readings.

Whichever method you select, it is a good idea to prepare this type of reading one or two months prior to your birthday. This is possible because a Solar Return Card Reading is not geographic-specific (not dependent on place) the way an astrological solar return reading would be. So it does not matter where you are currently residing or traveling to, since your location is not a factor in a card reading the way it is in an astrology reading. Therefore, the reading may be prepared months ahead, even if you don't know which city or state you'll be in on your actual birthday.

The last 60 days of your old year is for you to tie up loose ends or finish up projects or even set new goals for the new year. This makes it an excellent time to do a reading on your upcoming year, as you will be most receptive then to the new information coming in.

Once you have set up your Solar Return Reading, you can use the *Card Interpretation Section* of this handbook to look up the meanings of each card. the *Card Interpretation Section* of this handbook will allow you to interpret your reading regardless of which reading you are doing or whose techniques you are following.

The Art of Interpretation
♥ ♣ ♦ ♠ ♥ ♣ ♦ ♠

Beginning To Read

Well, all-righty then! Ready to dive right in? After you have selected a card deck and decided what type of reading you'd like to do, the next step is to form your question, lay out the cards and interpret them. Or, if you are doing a weekly reading, simply focus on the week you think you have planned ahead ("we plan, God laughs") and lay out your reading.

Remember to center yourself and focus your energies before you deal out the cards. Interpretation is where this handbook may be most helpful to you. Particularly if you are not used to combining the energies of the cards, the suits and the planets.

Here are some good general principles that apply to any reading:

Combine the meanings of ALL cards for the overall energy of the reading. For instance, in a weekly reading Mercury's card isn't always just about Wednesday (or your start day, whichever day of the week that might happen to fall upon). The events represented by the cards may happen on any day of that week.

I do not consider inverted cards to have a different meanings. *If a card appears "up-side-down" it is read exactly the same as "right-side-up."*

I know some card reading methods use a different interpretation for inverted cards (Tarot, for instance, as well as some others), and they see them as expressing negative, unbalanced or just different energies. That is not the case when reading using my Grandmother's method with standard cards. She taught me that the card meaning is the same, regardless of orientation. She even had a little rhyme for it:

"There's despair enough to go around, don't read the cards as upside-down."

OK, well, remember, I was only a little girl when she was teaching me! Rhymes helped me keep the rules straight. So, really, the only thing that might color a specific card's meaning are the cards appearing on either side of it. The cards affect one another and their meanings are often blended together (or at least considered) before making a prediction. And, believe me (or Gram!), that if negative energies need to be expressed in the reading, there are more than enough other ways to for the cards to express it.

The Summary Cards in a reading represent not only the overall energy of your question/week/month/year (depending on which reading you're doing), but perhaps the most important elements of that time frame. Even missed opportunities can be represented here.

If you throw a reading that doesn't make any sense at all, walk away. Do not try to read again for at least an hour. If this happens three times in a row, don't read at all that day. I call this one "bad juju." I think that sometimes there is just some bad energy hanging about, and until you get rid of it you don't mess with the cards. "Respect the energy." That's what Gram always told me. It's still good advice.

Don't read when you're ill. It takes energy to read—even for yourself. And when you're not well your energy is off, so your reading will be off too. In addition, you may drain yourself and that can make your health even worse. Just take some time to rest and conserve your energy until you are feeling well again.

If a card "jumps" out at you—falls out of the deck, or literally "jumps" into your hand as you shuffle—it's trying to get your attention! Read it. Consider it a "bonus" part of your reading. A "jumper" card is read independently of the other cards. It's like a special extra or bonus message. I don't assign it to a planet, but I suppose if you're looking it up in the handbook, use either the overall description of the card number (top of the card section) or the *Summary Card* (under the suit) would be your best bet in terms of help with interpretation.

Occasionally, my reading leaves me feeling dissatisfied in some peculiar way. I get the "willies" for some reason. I can't quite explain it. It's like I've missed something. So, rather than redo my entire reading, I just throw just one extra card. After I've read the initial cards in the reading, I'll say something like: "Universe: what did I miss?" Then I read the extra card. Kind of puts a "period" on it for me.

Blending The Energies

In order to interpret your reading—whether you are seeking information for one simple question or looking for information about the entire year—you will need to practice blending the energies of the card number with the card suit and the planetary ruler. This is the basis of ALL readings and it is where the true artistry of cartomancy comes into play. It takes patience, practice, and of course it doesn't hurt to bring just the teensiest bit of psychic ability into it. We all have some intuition. Practicing it makes it stronger. You will also have to thoroughly familiarize yourself with each and every card and their particular individual eccentricities (see the *Cards Section*).

Take Sevens, for instance. I think they can be some of the trickiest cards to read because they don't seem to have any middle ground. It's either the high road or the low road with Sevens, and there is not much road at all in between. It's either challenges or blessings, with no shades of grey.

For most of us mere mortals, if you have a week with several Sevens, it's fairly certain that you may be facing multiple challenges in life that week. However, while the cards can show you what is before you, what they cannot show you is how you will respond. That is your decision alone (thanks to free will) and can make all the difference. If you face up to your challenges willingly and do your best to handle them, you may actually be better off in the end. Sevens build character, after all, and they bestow great blessings once the lessons are learned.

In addition to free will, there is also the matter of planetary influence. Take the specific example of the 7 ♦ under Jupiter. The 7 ♦ shows lessons around prosperity or attitudes of abundance and can definitely present financial challenges. However, don't forget that the 7 ♦ is also known as the "Millionaire's Card" because once those lessons have been processed and learned, you are free to take the high road and transcend the problems. So 7s can actually be quite lucky for some. And the 7 ♦ under Jupiter is much more likely to be positive, than say, the 7 ♦ under Saturn. The only real danger under Jupiter would be the tendency to spend too much. Jupiter rules expansion and tends to live large, but an "embarrassment of riches" is a problem we should all have! If you use your 7 ♦ under Jupiter for generosity or charity, you're on the right track, because Sevens almost always require personal sacrifice.

The really important thing to take away from this is that ANY card can be a good one (yes, even that spooky 9 ♠!). The cards themselves don't represent good or bad, they represent choices—choices already made or choices yet to be made. We have free will for a reason.

Take, for example, the Three, Five and Seven of Diamonds. When new readers see these they tend to predict a lack of funds, but that isn't always true. After all, in some spreads the 7 ♦ can represent quite a fortune because it can indicate that the person has finally released their poverty consciousness. The 5 ♦ simply means a change of fortune, and the 3 ♦ shows financial decisions. All of these cards stand for money moving, money flowing out. In general, we say that the 5 ♦ is a small amount going out and the 9 ♦ is a large amount going out. And, of course, sometimes in life money does need to flow out. How would we obtain the goods and services needed to survive if this were not so? But when reading, do try to keep in mind that terms like "large" and "small" are relative. To a wealthy individual, $10,000 might be considered a mere pittance; but to a person of limited means, that same $10,000 might represent a fortune.

Yes, sometimes if there are many unstable cards grouped together, it can mean that finances are tight (or will be so if the current path is not altered). Or perhaps lessons regarding value need to be processed. But the cards themselves simply represent those lessons or point out themes we are working with in life. They either show where our past decisions have led us, or where current path will lead. Learning to make good choices is an important life lesson. Some of us are further along than others in life, but we are all working on something and the cards can be a valuable tool to help us navigate the path we've chosen.

Also, when reading keep in mind that, in general, odd numbers will indicate action—both good and bad—and even numbers will indicate stability. Again, this could be good or bad depending on the desired outcome... sometimes you want change/action when none is forthcoming. And sometimes too much stability or sameness means you are stuck in a rut.

For example: Twos and Fours promote stability with partners and the home; Sixes are about karma–reaping what has been sown (both good and bad karma); Eights offer protection and Tens offer success, or the fruits of your previous efforts. While Aces (Ones), Threes, and Fives indicate change or movement; Sevens indicate challenges or blessings; and Nines indicate endings or completions.

Following are just a few examples of specific cards and how you might use their special meanings in interpretation. This is by no means a complete list, these are just some typical cards you might come across when reading and how they might be interpreted.

Ace ♠ The Mystical Magical Card. The ruler of the deck and all ancient mystical and hermetical knowledge and wisdom. The symbol for Spade used to be an inverted leaf taken from the Tree of Knowledge. This represents sacred or divine information. In a reading, the Ace ♠ stands for initiation into mystical teachings or a higher state of being.

2 ♥ This engagement or "couples" card can indicate romance, marriage or honeymooners.

3 ♣ the writer's card. Also known as the "tall tale teller's" card if surrounded by negative energy, and can represent someone who exaggerates or stretches the truth.

4 ♥ This is the marriage or happy home card and indicates marriage and family.

5 ♥ or 9 ♥   These are cards of separation, and they can indicate a broken engagement or pending divorce. But "separation" can also mean that one partner is traveling (thus the couple is separated by distance). In a reading this generally refers to a change of heart or the end of the relationship, and sometimes that's a good thing!

5 ♠   The relocation or long-distance travel card. This card can also indicate a change in health or your daily work load.

7 ♦   This enigmatic card can either indicate poverty or riches, and it has more to do with your state of mind than the state of your wallet. When all financial karma has been dissolved, money is free to flow unencumbered and "la fortuna" rises, naturally, without effort or struggle. Of course, this doesn't explain why so many lottery winners end up unhappy! Perhaps receiving a large sum also has its own particular karma.

9 ♦   The bankruptcy card. Or, it may just indicate a time of large expenditures. This is really more about the cycles of prosperity in our lives than our bank balance. If we have put all our faith in money (if we are morally bankrupt), then this can mean we have bigger problems than our bank accounts.

9 ♠   The death card (although it is not always physical death); generally indicates grief or saying goodbye. This can also refer to other types of important endings or even purging the health. The Spades endings tend to be a bit more final (and intense) than some of the other suits.

J ♦   This is the gambler's card and can refer to an actual gambler or just someone who takes a lot of risks. It indicates someone who is comfortable with risk or speculation but can also manifest as a con-man because they can talk you out of a dollar pretty quick! Keep in mind, though, that no card is good or evil. The Jack of Diamonds indicates a high level of creativity with money. Used well, this could also be an inventor.

J ♠   This is the card of secrets, or the liar's card. It is also the card of the Druid or Priest, or anyone who can keep secrets and confidences. Negatively, this card can indicate someone who is unfaithful or who has many affairs, and positively, it can indicate someone who works with proprietary data and keeps his or her word.

Q ♥   The Mother Mary card. It represents the purest unconditional or spiritual type of love and selfless service to others. It can also indicate actual mothers and motherhood.

Keywords

The PLANETS: the energies and myths they personify

MERCURY ☿ *COMMUNICATION,* conversation, the mind, the intellect, writing, speaking, the details, being fleet of foot, quick, witty, sly, the writer, the teacher, the salesman, the trickster, Hermes, Messenger to the Gods

VENUS ♀ *LOVE,* romance, sensuality, attraction, desire, money, home, art, beauty, femininity, the model, the designer, the artiste, Freya or Aphrodite, Venus rising on the half-shell, The Goddess of Love

MARS ♂ *ENERGY,* drive, ambition, passion, sexuality, anger, aggression, knives, metal, blood, action, impatience, courage, flexibility, masculinity, the athlete, the fighter, the warrior, Ares, The God of War

JUPITER ♃ *EXPANSION,* excess, obesity, good fortune, blessings, generosity, the big picture, the sky's the limit, acting, the theatre, Santa Claus, humor, fun, travel, philosophy, world view, truth, Zeus, King of the Gods

SATURN ♄ *MATURITY,* responsibilities, adulthood, caution, pragmatism, prudence, calcification, the aging process, hard work, overwork, clockwork (being on time), achievement, the authority, the boss, Cronus, Titan—Son of Uranus and Gaia, and Father to Zeus

URANUS ♅ *CHANGE,* sudden revelation (or revolution), spontaneity, brilliance, flashes of insight, erratic, unpredictable, astrology, the occult, the strange or unusual, aliens, the inventor, Ouranos, God of the Sky

NEPTUNE ♆ *SPIRIT,* psychic vision, prophecy, sight, divine love, charity, compassion, cosmic consciousness, the afterlife, music, poetry, the ideal or idealistic, anything mystical, magical or ethereal, dream life, sleep, drugs, alcohol, addiction, water, Poseidon, God of the Sea

PLUTO ♀ *POWER,* personal transformation, death and rebirth, control, sexual abuse and healing, Tantric sex, intensity, drama, depth, challenges, large corporations and big business, the detective, the Guardian at the Gate, Hades, Lord of the Underworld

The Suits

HEARTS ♥ Hearts **FEEL.** They are intuitive, emotional, and relationship-oriented. If you were born a Heart you are meant to develop partnerships with others, and superficial relationships are your enemy. Only a heart that is true to itself can choose the right relationships and partnerships.

A Heart who lives in fear avoids relationships and loves no one.

CLUBS ♣ Clubs **THINK.** They also talk, speak, and communicate. Clubs make excellent teachers and librarians and are conversant and curious. Clubs are idea people who love to read and research, and meaningless data is their enemy. If you were born a Club you were meant to explore the world of thoughts and ideas. Eventually you have to figure out how to turn all that information into wisdom.

A Club who lives in fear
hides behind meaningless words or reams of data and says nothing.

DIAMONDS ♦ Diamonds **ACCRUE.** They are born knowing the value of a dollar and can attract wealth. "Value" is, in fact, a key word for them and debt is their enemy. Diamonds tend to be goal-oriented and know early in life what they want. If you were born a Diamond, you are meant to develop a personal set of values, which begins with valuing yourself.

A Diamond who lives in fear chases wealth but values nothing.

SPADES ♠ Spades **ACT.** Above all else, they "do." They represent actualization on many levels and their enemy is passivity. If you were born a Spade you were meant to take on the world! To get out there and experience life firsthand. Spades tend to be "hands-on." More than the other suits, Spades have access to hidden knowledge (the Spades symbol is an inverted leaf from the Tree of Life). Theirs is the responsibility to serve others and use the information well.

A Spade who lives in fear
hides out from the world and accomplishes nothing.

The Numbers

(both positive and negative keywords are included)

ZEROS: *FAITH*, all things are possible, hope, surprise, the leap of faith, the chameleon, the shape-shifter, the fool

ONES: *THE BEGINNING*, new beginnings, the start point, identity, self-improvement, independent, loner, isolation, self-focused, "me-first"

TWOS: *UNION*, partnership, unconversation, negotiation, agreements, contracts, togetherness, arguments, debates

THREES: *CHOICE*, creative, decisions to make, choices, indecisive, flighty, flibbertigibbets, worrying, complaints

FOURS: *STABILITY*, foundation, steady, solid, balanced, comfortable, dependable, predictable, complacent, rooted, stuck, self-satisfied

FIVES: *CHANGE*, movement, action, going somewhere, too much change too fast can upset the apple cart, scattering efforts to the 4 winds

SIXES: *KARMA*, dissolving or accruing, karmic lessons, past life people or events, no forward movement, dealing with something important before you can move on

SEVENS: *SACRIFICE*, challenges, obstacles, hidden blessings, lessons lived and learned, detachment, trans-personal, self-sacrifice, rising above.

EIGHTS: *POWER*, protection, able to overcome all obstacles and challenges, infinite knowledge, never-ending cycles, all roads lead home

NINES: *COMPLETION*, release, purging, graduation, the last of something, something flows out, to be finished, over or done, canceled, extinguished, divorced, trials and tribulations, challenges to be overcome, extremes: both spiritual heights and hellish depths, death, rebirth

TENS: *SUCCESS*, expansion, larger than life, big, many, lots of, winning. Sometimes too much of a good thing is wonderful and sometimes it's too hot to handle

ELEVENS: *YOUTH,* creativity, children or young adults, the student, community, the novice, the apprentice, youthful enthusiasm, persuasive, charming, salesmanship, immature, manipulative

TWELVES: *TEACHER,* mature, unconditional love, kindness, compassion, gentleness, the nurturer, the mother, smothering, clinging, over protective

THIRTEENS: *LEADER,* mature, responsible, fair, just, the father, the grown-up, the authority, the leader, bossy, bullying, controlling, lording power over others

About the Tens and Court Cards

The cards beyond 9 can all be reduced numerologically. That is, the 10, Jack, Queen, and King really represent 2 numbers. When we reduce a number we add its components together. So, the 10 would reduce as: 1 + 0 = 1. The Jack, being an 11, would reduce as: 1 + 1 = 2. The Queen (12) would reduce as: 1 + 2 = 3. And the King (13) would reduce as 1 + 3 = 4. These give an additional underlying value to each of the court cards, plus the 10.

So, for example, the underlying value for a 10 is a 1. This puts additional self-focus on the 10 and allows it to fully express itself in a grand way. This does not in any way detract from the original meaning of the Ten (success, expansion, etc.), but simply carries an additional emphasis on self-knowledge and the development of personal skills, talents and abilities. Tens truly want to be all they can be. And then some!

The underlying value for a Jack (11) is 2. This gives the Jack the ability to move in and out of partnerships quite easily. It also helps them to become excellent negotiators or salesmen, but it can also sometimes make them argumentative as well. At the very least they are effective debaters. Either way, watch out! Because—love him or loathe him—Jack is certain to be one charismatic, silver-tongued devil.

The underlying value for a Queen (12) is 3. The 3 strengthens the mental powers and allows the Queen to be an intelligent communicator and an excellent teacher.

The underlying value for a King (13) is 4. The 4 provides a firm foundation of support. A solid, steady base from which the King may build his kingdom.

Multiples

When things repeat in a reading, take note. Repetition is a message in and of itself. Notice when your reading has a lot of either the same suit or the same number. This is telling you what energies your week will be made of, or what you will be preoccupied with.

For instance, several Aces could point to many new beginnings, while Aces mixed with Fives show significant changes (relocation, new job, new family, etc.). Aces mixed with Spades or Diamonds could mean new clients at work.

Double Threes can mean "ships that pass in the night." Three's often indicate an "either/or" situation. Oftentimes we must make a choice at the Three as to what direction we should take. If there is much confusion about the direction; or if there is more than one person or circumstance involved in the direction, then it can be a hit or miss situation where the parties pass like ships in the night unbeknownst to one another. In other words, you can miss one another (or the boat, plane, cab etc) along your journey. Three's require choice. Once you have chosen your path, see where it leads you.

I have found that several Fives and Nines in one weekly reading mean that clients will cancel or be "no-shows." In other words there is a change of plans or endings. Friends may cancel plans or trips may be delayed.

Several Eights and Tens show a week of overcoming all troubles and succeeding despite challenges or set-backs.

Many Hearts show a week of interaction with family and friends. Many Diamonds show a preoccupation with finances; while many Clubs denote conversations, emails, phone calls, letters, paperwork, writing, etc. Repeated Spades can mean there is lots going on with your health or at work with coworkers/employees. Of all the suits, I have found that Spades are most likely to show physical activity. With multiple Spades, you are doing something, you are accomplishing something, you are active.

Many court cards (Jacks, Queens, Kings) show lots of people around you (all with their own opinions and agendas no doubt!).

Also, if you know the Birth Cards of yourself and your friends and family members, remember that they can sometimes show up in a reading when you will be having important interactions with them. Your Birth Card or Sun Card is defined by your birth date. Please see the section on **Birth Cards** to determine your Birth Card (or refer to the books in **the Recommended Reading List**).

Sample Readings
♥ ♣ ♦ ♠ ♥ ♣ ♦ ♠

You might think that a seasoned pro such as myself would never need to do a reading to foretell my own future. But there you would be woefully mistaken. For if "practice makes perfect" then I should be darn near invincible by now! Alas, such is not the case, and I do weekly or monthly readings for myself every year. Besides keeping me humble, it also allows me to continue my studies into the mysterious and fascinating world of Cartomancy.

One of my very favorite things about studying the cards is that you are never finished! It's like a book that writes itself new chapters every time someone approaches the end. The cards are a living, breathing language. And it continually surprises me to learn that they will always have new things to say.

So please allow me to share a few of my own personal readings. Here I offer 2 Weekly Reading samples plus one Simple Question Reading. Courage, beginners! Mastering the Simple Question Reading will come quickly, and before too long you'll be ready to try some Weekly Readings.

A Weekly Reading is a wonderful exercise for any reader. It allows you to experience first hand how the cards and planetary energies interact. So, let's begin with a dramatic sample Weekly Reading from my own personal notebook. I have also included a blank worksheet for you to record your own readings in **the Resources Section**, in the back of the book. Feel free to copy.

NOTE: I would normally lay out this reading with 8 cards straight in a row, Summary Card on top. I laid it out this way so it would fit on one page. As you practice more and more you'll likely develop your own style of layout for the cards.

Sample Reading 1 shows the German *Poker Deck* (Altenburger)

Kartenbilder: (©) 2016 ASSAltenburger Spielkarten; www.spielkartenfabrik.de

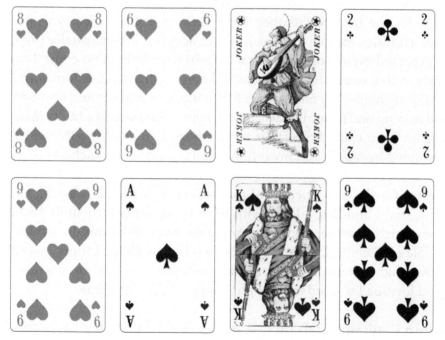

INTERPRETATION: *Sample 1—An Eventful Week*
The sample reading cards are read from left to right, and follow the planetary order from Mercury thru Pluto, Summary Card on top.

Mercury Card: 8 ♥ This card is about overcoming all challenges in communication with love, speaking your heart, and overcoming personal disappointment. Love flows from and to you thru words. Friends were extremely kind and caring during this difficult week, and they helped me overcome a transportation problem (getting around town is a Mercury thing).

Venus Card: 6 ♥ Plans canceled, a long-term relationship, karmic love or karma with loved ones, heartsick, balancing your emotions and home life. The 6 shows up under Venus when it's better to stay home than go out. I had a busy week planned originally, but as you will see, all plans were soon canceled.

Mars Card: JOKER! The energy you thought was there, may suddenly desert you. But run the race you thought you couldn't win anyway, hope for the best. Remember—just showing up is a victory in itself. Opportunities involve men or physical activity. Jokers usually predict unexpected events, or events that we will have little to no control over. Early in this week I had a serious fall down a flight of outdoor stairs—totally my fault—my hands were full, it was late at night, and it was dark and raining out. I should have known better, but I was in a hurry (Mars). The accident caused a serious hemorrhage in my left eye (bleeding—also ruled by Mars), and my retina tore and partially detached.

Jupiter Card: 2 ♣ Successful partnering with friends, sharing company, travel buddies, talking with friends. Benefits thru shared ideas, an expansive partnership, a fortunate meeting of the minds, groups of people of like mind, mental support, a fellow student. I think this card shows that I would find a fortunate partnership. And by a stroke of good fortune I was led to the right people at the right time.

Saturn Card: 9 ♥ Difficult loss, depression. Working hard at networking, firing someone, letting someone go, new people come with responsibilities—stick with those you already know, friends at work are hard to find, mixing business and pleasure must be done carefully. Losses under Saturn tend to be more difficult or more serious than under other planetary influences. Saturn also rules one's career path and achievement in general and what I worried about most after the accident was a loss of work. I feared losing clients because I needed to see in order to read the cards or interpret an astrology chart. Would I go blind and lose my business? In fact, I did not end up losing clients, and my "sight" was better than ever—it kicked in where my eyes failed. But sometimes the cards show us our fears so that, in facing them, we might avoid creating future problems for ourselves.

Uranus Card: Ace ♠ A sudden revelation, uncovering hidden or occult information, your secret "Ace-in-the-Hole" that pulls your fat out of the fryer! Aces under Uranus show hidden information coming to light. The retina is not that easy to see, as it turns out, and I had to undergo a series of tests by several different doctors to determine the extent of the damage. Having an "Ace in the Hole" means that there are hidden reserves—in this case it pertained to my health, but also to my ability to bounce back (by improving my outlook).

Neptune Card: King ♠ Intuitive success, hidden information benefits you, proprietary data, "for your eyes only," eye doctor, dreams of being at the top. It could mean heading up a metaphysical or spiritual business or it could also show caring for the rich and the poor equally. The King of Spades is someone at the top of his or her game, an expert. Through a complete stroke of luck (Joker) I ended up seeing one of the top retinal surgeons in the country. He saved my eye (and most of my vision). Neptune rules vision and sight, so a King of Spades here can, quite literally, represent an "eye specialist."

Pluto Card: 9 ♠ The "death" card. This card's themes include purging health habits, physical transformation and release, the aging process, life, death, rebirth—the cycle of life, processing loss or grief, being transformed by endings. Something has been completed and permanent change is at hand. Now, I will not lie, the 9 ♠ under Pluto is a serious card and it can, at times, indicate actual death. But it also means purging, releasing, and letting go--and what you're releasing with the 9 ♠ is not usually coming back. The Spade suit pertains to ones health. Perhaps it was a warning to me that the fall could have been fatal and that I needed to be more careful in the future. Or, perhaps it was just informing me that part of my sight had been permanently lost, which it was. But as I reflected upon it, I realized that what was "dying" was a way of life that was not supporting me. Nines turn up to warn about something ending, going away, or disappearing. And under Pluto, there has to be a change of some kind, a personal transformation. This accident almost cost me all my vision (or, one might use the term "sight," and it might stand for more than just my eyes!). I did not regain all my sight, but neither did I go blind. Also, I realized some of my health habits had to completely change going forward, and that I had to work on improving my balance and my overall health.

TOP: Summary: King ♥ This brings people power, and shows that a solid emotional base supports everything else in life. To say this was not one of my favorite weeks would be an understatement, but amazingly it did all work out in the end. Yes, I needed several months of recovery but I got through it. When reading the weekly cards I do tend to give a bit of extra weight to the summary card because it shows the end result, and when it's as good as the King ♥ it predicts a favorable outcome. The King ♥ carries within it a great deal of people power as well, and when my friends found out about my accident they rallied round and were truly helpful—getting me to and from doctor visits (I couldn't see, so I couldn't drive), sending cards, phoning, stopping by with "tea and sympathy" and making me aware that I was not alone. It was truly comforting to see such an outpouring of care and it did bolster my spirits.

Comments: Overall, this was a tough week and I found it difficult at times to stay calm and positive. Seeing those two Nines right off the bat was a bit off-putting. But I can see that the Joker card was trying to tell me that my attitude could either help or hinder me—my choice. Had I panicked or believed early on that there was no hope for improving my condition, I think I would not have fared as well. Staying calm, meditating and being surrounded by loving, caring friends all served to help me weather the storm. And having the King ♥ as the summary card also let me know that I would recover. Finally, remember that no matter how bad a reading looks, it represents only one week's time. It's good to know that each week we have another opportunity to improve things and make things right. Hopefully this one small example illustrates just how much information one can obtain through a "simple" weekly reading!

OK, well that sample reading showed a rather intense and eventful week. Next let's take a look at a sample reading for a rather more average week.

Sample Reading 2 shows the *Astronomical Card Deck* (Piatnik)

Piatnik: Printing of 1172 Astronomical card deck authorized by Wiener Spielkartenfabrik Ferd. Piatnik & Sohne, A-1140 Vienna, © by Piatnik Vienna 2016, www.piatnik.com

INTERPRETATION: *Sample 2—An Ordinary Week*

Note that the second sample reading is read in the same order as the first: from left to right, same planetary order (Mercury thru Pluto), Summary Card on top. You could probably just as easily place the Summary Card on the bottom, but I like to keep it in mind as I read because it affects (and should be blended with) every other card.

Mercury Card: 6 ♣ This card relates to the karma of communication and warns to think before speaking, to speak your truth, and to keep your word. Writer's block or stalled writing or research may occur. As this card also happens to be my own, personal birth card (the card for July 22nd), it indicates to me a week of focusing on my own individual goals. I started the week with a bit of writer's block and I was feeling kind of stuck. I was writing a book and a card class at the same time. Sixes under Mercury can mean that the flow of communication is largely internal, but in order to write or teach successfully you must find a way to make it external.

Venus Card: Jack ♦ Your charisma can work for you now, providing sales ability as well as marketing and financial creativity. I had been working on some creative ways to connect with clients and this week I managed to reach out more. I also expanded my marketing plan. Marketing is not something that comes naturally to me, so this required some creative thinking in an area I'm often puzzled about. I took good advice from a friend who excels at it and that made the difference. Know when (and who) to ask for help!

Mars Card: King ♣ This indicates the ability to successfully focus your attention in order to achieve your ambitions, channel your thoughts in one direction, and use your own drive or passion for success. It can also show working with successful men. I broke through the writer's block, got my class written and managed to write several chapters of my book. It might seem like a small thing to you, dear reader, but I was on top of the world! I also met with several business men at the top of their professions and received some really good advice about my own business.

Jupiter Card: 10 ♥ Surrounded by successful or highly placed people while socializing, which leads to success. Much of my business this week was with friends and people I knew socially, so it was easy to combine business with pleasure (not something I often get to do). As an added bonus I got out and about and had fun!

Saturn Card: 2 ♥ Speaking with maturity and love. This card is about showing up for one another, and just being there. It emphasizes a parent's love, or a mature union between two people, as we all must weather the challenges of love and partnership. There is also an emphasis on a durable love, a strong bond that is long-lasting. My daughter was having a difficult time this week, and so our talks were both serious and challenging. But the bond between mother and child is not a fragile one and it can withstand a good deal of stress without breaking. I had to remind myself of this several times during the week.

Uranus Card: 2 ♦ A partner's resources may be unpredictable or they may have a sudden windfall that benefits you. Or this could mean a gift, or a surprising offer of help. A friend received an unexpected bonus at work and decided to spend it all at my website! I was surprised and delighted.

Neptune Card: Jack ♠ Secret knowledge, channeling divine inspiration, following a spiritual guru. Dreaming of a work or health-related matter. I needed to come up with some creative ideas for card classes and my grandmother appeared to me in a dream and showed me how she would have taught the class. Needless to say, it was quite illuminating.

Pluto Card: 10 ♣ Challenged to be the best teacher, speaker or writer you can be; successful communications transform you. Your Pluto Card will often show where you face the biggest challenge in the week and I definitely struggled to write better. Because I didn't back down from the challenge or let the writer's block win, I succeeded in pushing past it (although I admit, I threw many pens across the room in frustration this week!).

TOP: Summary: King ♥ People power, leading others, being a successful parent or mentor to others, a solid emotional base supports everything else in life. A lot was going on in my family this week that required me to be the "grown-up" and have some heart-to-heart talks. That, combined with the writer's block, provided more than enough internal frustration. So, it was extra nice to have friends (K♥) around to remind me what a sense of humor looks like. They saved me from myself and made the week much more fun. They also allowed me to bounce some of my business ideas off of them and that proved to be invaluable.

Comments: As you can see, this week was rather more ordinary, more "business as usual" and less....let's see, how shall we put this....adventurous, perhaps? Well, at least I didn't fall down anything! I did start the week with some creative blocks, but I worked through them and was able to come out the other side, better and wiser. The more I managed to just "show up and open up" in my life, to the people, messages (and spirits?) around me, the better my writing became. So nothing terribly exciting happened, but it was a good week overall (and your Summary Card will often confirm this). And, unless you are a celebrity, this is likely to be the case for most of your weekly readings. For the rest of we "hoi palloi" a weekly reading can provide a surprising amount of detail even for an ordinary week. Hopefully these examples give you a sense of just how amazingly useful your weekly reading can be.

Pay special attention to multiples in your reading. This week I had multiple Jacks, Tens, and Twos. This showed me that success this week would require creative partnerships, which it did. I even managed to "partner" with my grandmother in the ethers! In this reading, the suits were fairly well mixed—all four of them showed up. In weeks where you have only one or two suits, your week will likely reflect those themes: People/Family issues for Hearts (Hearts Feel); Communication/Writing for Clubs (Clubs Think); Money/Values for Diamonds (Diamonds Accrue); and Work/Health for Spades (Spades Act/Do). Check the Keywords Section in the Handbook for more information on this.

Please note that although my creative blocks (indicated by the 6 ♣) occurred early in the week, this does NOT mean that the Mercury card will only be in effect for the 1st day of your week. Mercury represents the mind, communication, writing; and the type of creative block I was having was definitely Mercury-related. If I had been an artist, perhaps my block would have shown up under Venus; and if I had been a Musician, maybe Neptune would have represented it. In your readings all of the cards will affect one another and their energies must be read together. If you have difficult cards showing up during your week, check your Summary Card. If that card is good, then you are likely to overcome many of the more negative influences that might appear during the week. And if your Summary Card is also challenging, it may represent problems that take longer than a week to resolve.

INTERPRETATION: *Sample 3— A Single Question*

During this week I had to pick my friend up at the airport. Now, the airport in my town is tiny. It would literally be hard to lose someone there. Still, I had an odd feeling about it. The weather had been dicey that week, so perhaps her flight would be delayed or canceled?

I decided to do a quick reading that morning to put my mind at ease. Note that the meanings of the cards for this type of reading do not require a planetary interpretation.

When looking up the meanings of the cards for a single question, you can just use the interpretation under the **Summary Card.**

1st Card: 3 ♣ This card is for managing a variety of mental ideas all at once and/or channeling worry into productive creative output. Choosing none (or focusing on too many at once) may scatter your energies to the Four winds. Select the most worthy ideas now for further development. Pay attention to details or all is lost.

2nd Card: 3 ♥ This card is about multiple social engagements, relationships or networking opportunities, and deciding which ones to pursue. It is also about deciding between potential (or competing) love interests. Which party should I attend? Which paramour should I accept? Which conversations matter the most? Choose carefully or you may end up without a date!

3rd Card: 4 ♥ A time of emotional stability and a peaceful heart. Or a heart may be stuck in a rut, lost in familiar people and feelings. The difference is this: are you sticking with them or are you stuck with them? The answer makes all the difference.

Well, this was a relief at least. Having a stable card like the 4 ♥ at the end shows that we would make it home together after all. It's kind of like the "all's well that end's well" card. Still, I just didn't know what to make of those double Threes.

Comments: If you read the *Interpretation Section* on multiples, then you know that double Threes can sometimes mean "ships that pass in the night" –which is exactly what happened.

My friend's plane had arrived a bit early, while I was in the restroom, so we missed one another, literally, by moments. After waiting about 15 minutes in the waiting room, I finally inquired as to where the flight was and was told it had already landed and everyone had already deplaned! I raced to baggage claim, thinking she might still be there. No friend. Then I went back to check the restrooms. Nothing. All during this time my mind was racing and I was running around like a headless chicken. What if she thought I forgot her! (gasp!) What a terrible friend she would think me! Would she take a cab home then? The 3 ♣ can really get your mind racing in a million directions, but the 3 ♥ reminded me that this was not a stranger, it was someone I cared about, someone I knew well. So I stopped and thought to myself: "OK, you know her, you know how she thinks, where would she go?"

Finally it hit me, and I ran outside and there indeed was my friend, scanning the parking lot looking for my car.

Once reunited, we had a wonderful ride home (as promised by the 4 ♥). We stopped for lunch and she told me all about her wonderful trip to see her family. Crisis averted, friendship saved.

I know that this was a very simple question. But even with just three cards you can see how much of the story is really told. Once you master interpreting the cards and blending their energies, there is a wealth of information just waiting for you. And, by the way (just in case you were wondering...), if my friend's plane had been cancelled–or if she had missed the plane entirely–I probably would have thrown Nines. This signals an ending more permanent than just a minor delay. And if her flight had merely been delayed due to weather, I probably would have thrown Sixes. This is more like a temporary "Stop Sign," where things are often delayed, but not denied.

The Cards Section

♥ ♣ ♦ ♠ ♥ ♣ ♦ ♠

Gram's Golden Rules

As you use the Cards Section to assist in the interpretation of your card readings, please remember that what I've listed here are just some of the suggested meanings for each card. This manual is meant to be a living, breathing tool to assist you in your quest for truth. Use it as a starting place...a jumping off point to help you develop your own talents and abilities as a reader. Over time your own intuition will kick in and may suggest additional meanings to you. Heed them.

Always listen to your own internal guidance when reading for yourself or anyone else. And the more you read, the more likely it is that your intuition will begin to grow in strength. This is quite common, and some of you may even begin to see or sense things as you read, or even begin to hear messages. This, of course, is in addition to any of the meanings you read here in this section; and you will find that your intuition will add to your overall ability to interpret the reading accurately.

After you have practiced reading for your family and friends (hopefully for at least a year), some of you will go on to read for clients. To those who are considering becoming professional readers, I offer my grandmother's Golden Rules (which I still use today):

1) Don't Make Decisions for Others
2) Trust the Message
3) Never Lie (although, sometimes it's OK to keep stuff to yourself)

When reading for clients, remember that your only obligation is to deliver the message as you receive it. Some messages may seem confusing to you and you won't understand them. That is perfectly OK, because the message is not for you. You are not the message, you are simply the phone line.

Sometimes you may even think that you are "making stuff up" in your own head. When messages first start coming in, this is a normal reaction to have. Trust the message and deliver it. Time and experience will prove to you that you didn't just "make it up."

Also, you are not responsible for whether or not someone actually heeds the messages or makes decisions around them. Readers are not supposed to make decisions for others. Readers simply convey information. What others do with that information is up to them and trying to influence them (beyond delivering the message) is interfering with their free will.

When we make decisions for people we take on their karma as well. Trust me when I say: avoid this if you can. Never lie to the client.

I once heard my grandmother tell a particularly difficult client: "Well, I could lie to you, but then I'd have to charge you double." Gram had a great sense of humor, but what she meant was that it wouldn't be worth it to her to lie to a client because she knew the true cost of such a foolish mistake.

Naturally, if you have information of a sensitive nature to convey, or if you suspect that the message you are about to deliver will upset your client, do be kind. Always. Think about how you would want someone to speak to you about a difficult topic. Kindness is a vastly underrated quality today, I think.

And, again, *NEVER* lie!

You can keep something to yourself once in awhile if it seems as though the client is just not able to hear it at that moment. This is because you should never push past what the client is able or willing to accept. In difficult cases, you must trust that if your client is meant to get the message, he or she will return for it...but never, ever lie.

Always, always, always follow your own gut. I have had many clients who begin their reading by saying to me "I want to know everything—the good and the bad and the ugly—everything!"

But most of the time "everything" is not what I tell them, because most clients have no idea just how much a reader can see, and even if they did, they are not actually as prepared as they think they are to hear "everything."

When I was very young, I remember a reading my grandmother did for one of her best friends. Her friend had come to her to ask a very specific question. She wanted to know if her husband was cheating on her. She said she wanted to know everything, so my grandmother told her everything. Names, places, when, how often, how long, etc.....you get the picture. "Everything" and then some was told...it was ugly. I remember actually being scared. The woman didn't believe my grandmother and threw the cards in her face! They had a terrible row. Finally, she screamed that Gram was crazy and left in a huff. They never spoke again. But Gram had been right, about everything. She was scary that way, and very accurate.

A few weeks later we heard about the divorce. It was quite the scandal in their little neighborhood. Soon after, the woman moved away and my grandmother lost a friend.

Should my grandmother have told "everything?" Well, she was an Aquarian, so I guess that type of blunt honesty was part of her make-up. She was just answering her friend's question, after all, so she didn't really do anything wrong.

I know that she had always disliked her friend's husband and felt that her friend deserved to be treated better, so perhaps she felt that her friend was better off knowing.

But I think that I would have answered that same question a bit differently. I, too, would have told the woman that her husband was unfaithful—yes I would have. She did ask and she was entitled to know. But I also would have made sure to tell her about the next man she was going to meet, the children I saw them have, and how happy they were going to be after all was said and done. I would have especially mentioned how much better her life would become, once she let go of this wrong one, so that she was free to meet the right one. That's what I would have said. But then again, I'm a Cancer, not an Aquarian!

And what would you have said? Think about it. Should you decide to become a Reader, how you answer questions will be more important than you realize.

So, follow the rules, and to my Grandmother's very wise rules, I will add one more of my very own: ***Keep Your Lips Zipped.*** As readers, we are privy to some very private information, and we have an ethical duty to honor the trust clients place in us and to keep things to ourselves. This is particularly important if you read for multiple members of the same family. As you might imagine, family members are curious and concerned about one another and they will quite naturally want to know how their sister, brother, wife, husband, daughter, son's (etc.) reading went. Which, of course, you must NEVER EVER tell them.

Clients may tell anyone they like the complete details of their readings, but *you* (as reader) must not. And no, you can't even hint about it, even if it is particularly juicy.

My standard response when one client asks about another is "Ask him (or her) yourself." You know, I have often thought that if I had a readings tent at a local Renn Faire it would have a sign over the door that read: "What Happens in the Tent Stays in the Tent." 'Nuf said?

4) *Zippeth thy Lippeth.*

The Search Function in the Digital Version

Many card readers travel from place to place to do readings. If you download the digital version of The Mystical Card Reading Handbook (and this is useful for those of you who prefer to travel with a laptop instead of a book), one very helpful tool available to you is the ability to search for exactly the card you need.

For example, let's say that you are doing a weekly reading and you throw the Ten of Diamonds for your Venus card. In the SEARCH box (in the upper right corner of your screen), you would simply enter: "Ten of Diamonds" (include the quotation marks). Then hit the RETURN key. This will automatically take you to the page describing the 10 ♦. If there is more than one occurrence of the 10 ♦, multiple choices will appear on the left side of your screen. Simply click on the one you want. This can be a real time-saver when you are first learning how to interpret your reading, when you will likely need to look things up more frequently. The digital version of the book is available on my website:

ourcosmicdance.com

Jokers

♥ ♣ ♦ ♠ ♥ ♣ ♦ ♠

The Use of Jokers

As an individual birth card, the Joker refers to people who follow their own rules. They act like a law unto themselves. They can either be chameleons and shape-shifters or fools. They often appear to be all things to all people, and as such are good actors, able to project their will outwardly. In the deck of 52, the Jokers make 54 (if you use them both) and they represent all suits.

In readings, the Jokers are considered as zeros, although not in the sense of "the absence of" but rather more in the sense of "all things are possible" because choices have yet to be made (this might be compared to the Fool card in the tarot deck).

At the Joker stage of things, everything is still a "potential" reality and the primary meaning here would be the concept of hope. One must cultivate hope for the future in order to look forward to it at all, or to manifest the best possible outcome. Not every Reader uses Jokers in their readings—including them is a personal choice—but if you do use them, you will find it helpful to use them consistently.

When I include the Joker in my readings, I generally try to see it as either a wild card—meaning all things are still possible—or as a harbinger of hopeful things to come.

But sometimes the Jokers warn us of unpleasant surprises as well. That does happen. So I call it my Halloween Card (as in "Trick or Treat"). Of course, if every day were a walk on the beach we wouldn't learn much, right? But either way, it tells me that the situation at hand is not yet decided and—more importantly—that I may play a crucial role in the outcome of things by simply paying deliberate attention, thereby taking immediate advantage of any wild card opportunities that suddenly appear, and also by hoping for the best.

Sometimes the Joker indicates an event or situation that you cannot stop. In that case—and especially if the event is negative in nature—if I can remain positive, at least I will have done my part to mitigate the extent of the negativity. Not all things are within our control, after all. But we can control how we choose to react to such events.

I have to tell a true story here, of a weekly reading I did for myself one December close to Christmas, in which the Joker appeared under Mercury. During that week, my phone just mysteriously stopped working altogether. As you might imagine, this was a problem because 80% of my business is conducted on the phone and I had readings scheduled. But instead of panicking, I chose to see it as a temporary opportunity to just "be still" and I spent the day meditating.

The next morning a package arrived from a friend containing a brand new phone. It was her Christmas gift to me. You know, you just can't make this stuff up. When the universe wants you to communicate, a way will be provided! If we can just "keep calm and carry on" all will be well. That is the true message of the Joker.

Joker

Mercury The message you waited for may not arrive, the call or letter is lost. But there may be other options. Keep hope in your voice and in your thoughts, use hopeful language, write your heart out, make the call–even if it's a long shot. Opportunities involve your ideas–launch them. Surprising correspondence follows.

Venus The love you counted on (friends, family, etc) might abandon you for the time being. But hope does spring eternal. Keep love alive in your heart, believe in the best for family and friends, opportunities involve women. Say yes to social invitations, take a chance, talk to her. Loved ones may yet surprise you. "Beauty will save the world."

Mars The energy you thought was there, may suddenly desert you. But run the race you thought you couldn't win anyway, hope for the best. Remember, just showing up is a victory in itself. Opportunities involve men of action or physical activity. Passion surprises you. Take a chance–talk to him.

Jupiter The trip doesn't come off as expected. But keep your bags packed anyway. Plan for future vacations. You never know. An attitude of gratitude takes you farther. Keep positive friends around you now. Opportunities involve travel, education, or like-minded companions. An adventurous journey in uncharted waters may surprise you.

Saturn You may not get the job. And you may be down, but you're not out unless you don't get up! Keep hope alive at work. This may be one of those times when the guy they hired over you doesn't work out and you get the job anyway. Opportunities involve work and your own efforts to succeed. What you can still achieve depends on you. Focus on what you can do, not what you can't.

Uranus Hope may actually come as a surprise now (or through surprising channels), but it's still in there. Take advantage of serendipitous opportunities. Remember, they are only opportunities if you can see them as such. Act quickly. What happens without warning may surprise you, but it doesn't have to stop you.

Neptune The prayer seems to go unanswered. But hope has not deserted you! Silence (or "not now") does not always mean "no." Sometimes it means "maybe later." Guard your "sight" (and your eyes) from negative images. Don't let others drain you. Don't believe everything you hear, but do take positive psychic messages to heart. Opportunities involve your spiritual life and your ability to see angels. "Your eyes may surprise!" Believe in your own path and stick to it no matter what.

Pluto Hope lives deep within your darkest hour but getting to it may be an intense experience. Hang on and keep diving. Opportunities involve the ability to transform the negative into the positive (or the ability to successfully navigate the dark side). Your own dark side may surprise you. But then, so will your ability to heal it. Believe in your own truth. Embrace it, live it, then transform it into what you want it to be.

SUMMARY: Pay attention now because surprises or changes beyond your control are in store. While we can't always control or even foresee all that will happen to us, we can control how we react to it. The Joker tells us to keep our footing regardless of how rocky the path. If you channel your "inner mountain goat" you may just reach the summit after all. And always hope for the best. Who knows? Keep a positive outlook and you may be pleasantly surprised. *Keep calm and carry on.*

BIRTH CARD: The only birthday for the Joker is December 31st. If the Joker is your Birth Card, you have a great deal of freedom. You have been dealt a "Wild Card" by life and may become the chameleon if you so choose. But whether you decide to live in the shadow or the sun, you will live by your own rules, and may become either a maverick or a cautionary tale. A Trickster to be sure, you have a lifetime of unlimited possibility ahead of you. How will you use it? You may just surprise yourself (and others) with what you can do. Keep your faith...and your eyes on the prize.

The Aces represent the start or beginnings of things, and conditions surrounding the startup/meet-up period. They can foretell the "firsts" in life: first love, first kiss, first job. They may indicate that an experience is being had for the first time and they may be telling you that something is only going to last a short time (one day only, a one night stand, a brief affair).

Or they may show you something that is unique or "one" of a kind. They also represent what is brand new and can therefore indicate birth or pregnancy. At the Ace stage of things seeds are planted, but only time will tell whether they will produce a harvest or not.

Mercury Hearing news of family, a meeting of the heart and mind, first words, words of affection, the beginning of a new relationship, pillow talk, love letters, letting love speak. Finding your heart.

Venus A budding romance or friendship, a single rose, first love, first kiss, new home, pregnancy, the birth of a new baby girl. Someone new likes you!

Mars A passionate or sexual attraction to someone new, a one-night stand, pregnancy, the birth of a new baby boy. Someone new wants you!

Jupiter New friendship or love that expands one's horizons, travel with someone new or meeting up with someone new on the road.

Saturn Working hard at networking, new people come with responsibilities, new friends at work, mixing business and pleasure. A labor of love, tilling the soil, nurturing the land, growing vegetables, tree hugging.

Uranus A sudden meeting or appointment. Erratic, unpredictable or just plain exciting people pop up, a friend surprises you with a visit, an unexpected pregnancy (surprise!).

Neptune A new spiritual or psychic friend, a new vision of love, the first impression, the initial gut-reaction, a one-time love affair, a dream comes true.

Pluto A depth of feeling, an intense new person enters your life. An important new start, love, or friendship transforms you. A catalyst of some kind opens your heart.

SUMMARY: The theme of the reading is new love. This is a time of emotional renewal, a love reborn, new habit patterns, new beginnings, new pathways, self-focused, concentrating on one's own particular interests. A time to welcome someone new into your life. Important "firsts" of some kind. Finding new ways to express love or to attract love to you. New friends, new loves. Birth with all its potential. The beginning of something or someone important in your life.

BIRTH CARD: If the Ace ♥ is your Birth Card, you wear your heart on your sleeve. Your lifetime will be filled with the discovery of new emotions, and your ability to feel them and then find ways to express them will be a big part of your life's path. You will experience yourself primarily though your feelings and will spend your life getting to know just what it takes to hear your own heartbeat. Beware of either giving your heart away too easily or living in the mirror and missing out on the people who love you. Be true to your heart. Emotional "firsts" (like your first love!) along with emotional growth and self-development will be important experiences.

Mercury A letter, email or phone call from a new place, studying a new subject, news, something new to say, letting your ideas be heard, starting the conversation (or starting over), the birth of your ideas. Finding the words.

Venus Studying art, learning in the home, book lover, beautiful new words or ideas, talking with friends and family, making a new friend.

Mars Passionate or assertive communication, an intellectual starting place, being excited about the conversation.

Jupiter A lucky break, A big new idea. Positive new information or ideas, happy news, a letter or call from far away, studying something new, classes just beginning, a new student, the professor or teacher appears. A new agreement.

Saturn Difficult communication, sad or disappointing news, new ideas may be hard to come by, struggling for the right words. Saying something—even when you're not sure just what to say. Planning the layout.

Uranus Sudden or surprising news, brilliant new ideas, new information or concepts, a light bulb goes off over your head (just like in the cartoons), suddenly just "knowing," inspiration strikes.

Neptune Hidden news comes to light, a new psychic message, dreaming new ideas into life, a single thought becomes real.

Pluto Intense new plans or ideas, in-depth research, new ideas that transform you in some way, manifestation using the power of the mind.

SUMMARY: The theme of the reading is new thought. This is a time of mental renewal, where the theme is communication and the birth of new ideas, a brand new way of looking at something important. Once you realize that everything begins with a single thought, your thoughts will help manifest your reality.

BIRTH CARD: If the Ace ♣ is your Birth Card, your ideas are always foremost in your thoughts, and communicating them will be a big part of your life's path. You will spend much of your life in the collection of facts and data, and in seeking answers to your many questions. You live in a world of the mind where reason and rational thought dominate the landscape. But beware of living in the library and missing out on real world experience. Be true to your ideals. Intellectual "firsts" (like your first book!) and the development of your mind will be important experiences for you.

♦ *Ace of Diamonds* ♦

Mercury A quick turn-around or profit, a new client, a new job or project, a temporary assignment, your ideas pay off now, the beginning of a new financial agreement, the first paycheck. Finding the resources.

Venus The first dollar, making money from home, working with family, purchasing something of beauty or value. A beautiful new home.

Mars Excitement for a new job, motivation for making money, an enthusiastic collector, passion and energy for a new start-up venture.

Jupiter A fun new job or opportunity, expanding your new business, getting your foot in the door, charity work, winning a scholarship.

Saturn A new position of responsibility or hard work on a new project. Patience is required for any new money-making venture now, as generating funds takes time and effort. Working hard for your paycheck, starting at the bottom (or starting from scratch) and working your way to the top. Purchasing land.

Uranus An unexpected windfall, an unusual offer or project, a forgotten payment turns up, suddenly finding something of value, a treasure hunt, alone with your money.

Neptune Financial liquidity, buying the boat, dreaming of future prosperity, the start of your financial dreams, a new metaphysical business, a new charity or philanthropic undertaking, financial gifts, the first of its kind, a one-day only psychic fair.

Pluto A brand new financial life, an important new job, an intense or in-depth beginning, transforming your idea of success, the rebirth of prosperity and abundance.

SUMMARY: The theme of the reading is new money. This is a time of new financial ventures, financial renewal, where the theme is the birth of new projects or the discovery of something of value. Exploring and assessing one's own personal worth. A brand new way of evaluating.

BIRTH CARD: If the Ace ♦ is your Birth Card, your financial status will consume much of your time and energy. Developing your own personal core value system, and knowing what is truly valuable to you personally, will play a big role in your life's path. You want to calculate exactly how much your time is worth, both literally and metaphysically. But beware of living in the counting house all of the time! Know what's important and be true to your values. Financial "firsts" (like your first paycheck!) and the development of your own personal value system will be important experiences.

♠ *Ace of Spades* ♠

The Ace ♠ is set slightly apart from the rest because it is the one card that rules over the entire deck. It represents the very beginning of all ancient and esoteric mystical knowledge, which can be obtained by careful study of the card system of prediction. The Spade symbol represents an inverted leaf–a leaf taken from the Tree of Knowledge or the Tree of Life, which preserved sacred and divine information.

    If you look carefully at your deck of cards, you will most likely notice that the Ace is decorated with special flourish (at least in most standard decks). Long ago it was foretold that of all the cards in the deck, only the Ace of Spades would be honored by special decoration.

Many card companies over the years have tried to decorate other cards, but most of those decks do not survive for very long. In a reading, the A♠ can stand for initiation into higher mystical teachings.

Mercury The beginning of an important new job or project, getting the ball rolling, an important conversation or new idea, letting your voice be heard. Learning esoteric or mystical information, specialized knowledge, knowing a secret, metaphysical truth revealed. Finding the time.

Venus A powerful new love, or secret affair. Pregnancy, birth, a new health regime. A new home or a new home office. A make-over, creating a new physical look.

Mars A passionate or sexual attraction, tantric sex, a new workout or energy for creating a healthy new lifestyle, a new exciting project at work that requires high energy.

Jupiter Travel to exciting new places, an unfamiliar path, secret teachings. Studying something new and exciting, declaring a new major.

Saturn A new job or career path, new property, breaking new ground. Being true to your ideals, responsibilities surrounding important knowledge or information, new health challenges, needing some alone time.

Uranus A sudden revelation, uncovering hidden or occult information, your secret "Ace-in-the-Hole" that pulls your fat out of the fryer! An unusual health matter requires more investigation.

Neptune An Important new psychic vision, seeing with new eyes (or needing new glasses), channeled information, inner healing, predicting the future.

Pluto A deep or intense new job or project, starting over, finding a transformational way to serve others, a brand new path. The beginning of all life. Pinocchio becomes a real live boy.

SUMMARY: The theme of the reading is new work. This is a time for the renewal of one's health, where the theme is "body as temple." Perhaps you are discovering something important now—either about your physical self or your spiritual self. This may also be a time for starting work that will be of service to others, the birth of the esoteric way of life, or finding one's true path. An important revelation may be received. Life begins (or begins again).

BIRTH CARD: If the Ace ♠ is your Birth Card, you are destined to become a "seeker" of knowledge in some chosen field, and this will play an important role in your life's path, but you will not know things in the way the other suits know things. Yours is a more intuitive path, and once you have married the facts and data with your natural intuition, you will begin to approach wisdom. Be true to your own special purpose and walk your own individual path, even when you walk alone. Physical "firsts" and developing and maintaining excellent health will also be important experiences. You are seeking "true north" and a purpose that only you might be able to truly understand, so make sure to select only projects worthy of that purpose. More may be expected of you at times than other cards, and this is because the Ace ♠ rules the deck. The power in this humble little card is often surprising, but beware of taking your power for granted. Use your enhanced knowledge and intuition to act in defense of others, and along the way, *never underestimate the power of just being nice!*

The Twos represent partnerships and agreements between parties. Pairing, sharing, co-operation, needing another to achieve completion are all important concepts along their journey through life.

Above all else, Twos stand for union. But all Twos will be deeply involved in the opinions and feelings of others to some extent, and so this can also represent debating, arguing, or pitting themselves against "the other," whoever and whatever the other may be. In this respect they could be prize fighters facing off in a boxing ring, or lawyers doing battle in court. "It takes two to tango" and two to marry (and let's not forget two to argue).

Twos present opportunities to see where we need to unite with one another–not just to survive but to thrive. No man is an island.

♥ Two of Hearts ♥

Mercury Heartfelt words, love letters, two of a kind, intimate communication, speaking your heart, sharing your feelings, listening to friends and loved ones, a quick visit from family.

Venus Peas in a pod, pillow talk, attracting a mate, being in love, an engagement, the honeymoon, creating family, making friends, sharing your heart (or giving it away), sharing space.

Mars Passionate love affair, romantic sex (or a quickie—your choice), a heated exchange, a strong desire for love or companionship, desiring family, putting your heart into it, sharing your passion (or your bed).

Jupiter Love blossoms, your love life expands, benefits or blessings thru others, friends and family are supportive, people come to your aid, people wishing you well.

Saturn Taking romantic commitments seriously (or to the next level), caring for—or being responsible to—another, speaking with maturity and love, showing up for one another, being there. A parent's love, a mature union. Weathering the difficulties of love and partnership. A love that is durable and long-lasting. A strong bond.

Uranus Lightning strikes, opposites attract, taking a sudden liking (or disliking) to someone, eloping, strong emotional reactions, knowing how the other guy feels, empathy.

Neptune Bedroom eyes, dreamboat, an ideal love, a clandestine affair, sharing a dream, seeing through the eyes of love, a spiritual partnership, doing favors for another with no expectation of return.

Pluto A deep or intense love that challenges you to be the best you can be, an obsession, your mate can make or break you, transformation because of love.

SUMMARY: The theme of the reading is a union of hearts. This is a time of personal partnerships with family and friends, togetherness, a marriage based on love, passion and friendship. Important people enter; bonds are formed. Or differences of feeling can cause arguments or emotional distance.

BIRTH CARD: If the 2 ♥ is your Birth Card, personal partnerships (marriage, business partner, best friend, etc.), and the way in which you relate to them, will be a major part of your path. And sharing your feelings with others won't always be easy. But whether loving or fighting with them, just finding those special people–the ones you can share your heart with in life–will play the most important role for you. One of your life lessons will involve the ability to reach an emotional compromise within your most meaningful relationships.

♣ *Two of Clubs* ♣

Mercury Discussions, debates, agreements between parties, signing on the dotted line, sharing ideas, finally getting through to someone (or them to you), a "study buddy."

Venus Sharing ideas with a partner or friend, working and talking with women, friendly negotiations, sharing art and beauty, a gabfest.

Mars Disagreement or passionate discussions, energetic teamwork, working and talking with men, high-energy negotiations, the interview, sharing a passionate mental exchange, "mental gymnastics."

Jupiter Successful partnering with friends, sharing company, travel buddies, talking with friends. Benefits thru shared ideas, an expansive partnership, a fortunate meeting of the minds, groups of people of like mind, mental support, a fellow student.

Saturn Long-term agreements, signed contracts, partnership negotiations. Partners may be mature and more experienced now, serious meetings with professionals and those in charge, government paperwork. Partnership may be difficult or may just require extra effort on your part. Speak clearly and responsibly. Take your time to avoid miscommunication or argument.

Uranus Sudden news, an unexpected partnership, a fast agreement. Discussing astrology or other metaphysical topics, sharing unusual or innovative ideas, brainstorming, inspiring one another to think outside the box.

Neptune Spiritual or psychic partnership, sharing music/poetry/theatre, a duet, uncovering hidden fears or phobias, dealing with mental stress or anxiety.

Pluto Communication with a partner or friend could transform or inform you, deep talks, important conversations, a challenging discussion or argument leads to enlightenment, a very important idea. A spiritual partnership.

SUMMARY: The theme of the reading is the union of minds. This is a time of mental partnerships, the marriage of ideas and philosophies, combining several ideas, communicating, networking, and sharing information. Learning where you really stand through discussions with another. The joining of like minds, or divisions and debates based on different ideologies. Will you choose to focus on the differences or the similarities?

BIRTH CARD: If the 2 ♣ is your Birth Card, communicating with others will be a major part of your life. But whether arguing, debating or just having an intelligent conversation, finding people of like-mind to share your ideas with will play an important role for you in some way. Honing your ideas by discussing them with others is necessary in order to fully develop them. One of your life lessons will involve intellectual compromise and the ability to "agree to disagree" within all of your most important unions.

✦ *Two of Diamonds* ✦

Mercury A financial partnership or agreement, financial advice, sharing valuable information with another, a quick sale or transaction, a fast buck.

Venus A prosperous partner, marrying for money or security, a shared system of values, working with a family member or having coworkers who seem like family as in "the office family," working with women.

Mars Putting energy into financial deals or partnerships, financial backing, an ambitious couple, partnership agreements (or disagreements) with men, financial negotiations.

Jupiter Generosity, sharing resources with a friend or partner (or them with you), financial support, sharing travel or educational costs.

Saturn Financial assistance from an authority figure (like a parent or the government), being aware of all financial responsibilities in relationships or in partnership agreements, a loan (with strings or conditions). Make sure you can pay it back!

Uranus The finances of a partner may be erratic or unpredictable now or a sudden windfall benefits both of you, a gift, a surprising offer of help.

Neptune Developing a higher value system, compassion, financial partnerships with spiritual or metaphysical people.

Pluto Intense or complex financial arrangements with others, control issues with money, financial debt, forgiving someone else's debt can transform your own life.

SUMMARY: The theme of the reading is a union of values. This is a time of financial partnerships, mergers, or negotiations. You will need to decide based on your own personal values, because sticking with them is more likely to bring success. Sharing valuable information (or others sharing with you). Sticking up for your personal values, or arguing over money. Learning that there are more important things in life.

BIRTH CARD: If the 2 ♦ is your Birth Card, forming financial partnerships with others will be a major part of your path. Your net worth will always be of interest in any partnership agreements, however it's joint security that you are really seeking. But pauper or king, in-debt or well-off, it's finding partners who can share your values in life that will play the most important role for you. One of your life lessons will involve knowing which values you can compromise on and which you can't, within your most valuable mergers.

Mercury A quick but meaningful conversation, a temporary partnership, meeting of the minds, co-operation, collaboration, work meetings.

Venus Partnering with women, dating someone at work, working from home, a home office, working with family, care taking.

Mars Working with men, passionate partnership, martial arts/athletics, fighting, arguing or having sex (or both, makeup sex?), taking action, taking the initiative in your partnership.

Jupiter Happily coexisting, the buddy system, blessings thru another, the support of coworkers, excellent health, expansive work relationships.

Saturn Partnership that requires compromise, meeting with health professionals, partnering with a pro, a long-term partnership, a real estate deal.

Uranus Sudden collaboration or unusual networking ideas, changing partners, odd couples, "going" for it, spontaneous plans.

Neptune Spiritual partnership, meeting with a psychic, charity work, getting lost then found, swimming for health, water therapies, sailing with a friend. "Two if by sea."

Pluto Intense partnership, cooperation and compromise may just transform the situation and improve things, a powerful (or obsessive) working partnership, a joint project or purpose. Seeing a vision of your healthiest self, then doing what it takes to get there. Powerful sexual union, Tantra.

SUMMARY: The theme of the reading is unity, pure and simple. This is a time of physical partnerships, the marriage of sex and love, using sex to settle differences. Partnerships to improve health and well-being—of yourself or the planet. You may also find someone to unite with for a cause. Partnerships or rivalries at work.

BIRTH CARD: If the 2 ♠ is your Birth Card, working partnerships or joint projects will be a major part of your life. Finding someone who helps support your health goals will also be important. But whether finding a kindred spirit who can share your purpose in life, or finding someone to fight with, partnerships will play an important role for you in some way. One of your life lessons will involve compromising for the sake of teamwork within your most in-depth projects.

Threes

♥ ♣ ♦ ♠ ♥ ♣ ♦ ♠

The Threes represent multiple choice or divergent paths. Do I go this way or that? You come to a fork in the road and a choice must be made, but before you choose you may vacillate, go back and forth, ponder, freeze or just end up being fickle. Trying to go in two directions at once can be quite the challenge!

Threes can also represent where we are extremely busy. Whether running here and there, or involved in multiple relationships, conversations and projects, they are variety itself and bring some much needed spice and creativity to life.

When you see Three think: choice, fork in the road, several, more than one, multiples, busy, many balls in the air. On a higher level, the threes represent the concept of Triple Goddess (Maiden, Mother, Crone) or the Holy Trinity (Father, Son, Holy Spirit); and the triune principal of divinity.

♥ *Three of Hearts* ♥

Mercury Lots going on with the people in your life, emotionally unsettled, fickle, choosing between two friends or lovers, a choice needs to be made, taking sides, be true to you.

Venus Variety or fickleness in love, many social engagements or invitations at once, lots of visitors. Deciding between two loves? Your heart already knows which one you want. Listen to it.

Mars Energetic pursuit of love, out on the town, looking for connection, playing the field, "two's company...three's a crowd" (or a party). Laughing and crying at the same time.

Jupiter Social growth and opportunity, meet and greet, networking in social settings (like parties or conventions or even the classroom), telling the truth about how you really feel.

Saturn A hard heart or a heart divided, worrying over lost love or love from the past (the "one who got away"), a difficult decision regarding friends or family, house hunting.

Uranus Many eclectic people, making an impromptu "choice of the heart." Suddenly knowing who should stay and who should go. But in the meantime, lots of friends show up and want dinner–oh, just order out and save yourself some stress. P.S.–International cuisine works well now.

Neptune Romantic fantasy, lots of fish in the sea. Feeling drained by giving too much: compassion may be needed by more than one person at a time. Who gets your love? The one who needs it most. Spiritual truth. Intuition in love.

Pluto Important people, challenged to meet everyone's expectations. You can't please all the people all of the time. And, newsflash: not everyone will love you! The loving and healing power of choice. Pushing the boundaries of relationships.

SUMMARY: The theme of the reading is choices in love, or the choices made because of love. This is a time where you will need to decide between multiple social engagements; relationships or networking opportunities; and deciding which ones matter. Also deciding between potential (or competing) love interests. Which party to attend? Which paramour to accept (or pursue)? Which conversations matter most? Answer carefully or you may end up without a date.

BIRTH CARD: If the 3 ♥ is your Birth Card, emotional decisions will be a major part of your life path in some way. At some point you may need to choose which life or business partner to select (which proposal to accept?) and your choice may have far reaching consequences. In all relationship matters, it will be important to listen to your heart. But beware of becoming fickle, or of making no decision at all, thereby abdicating your right to choose (and ultimately experiencing) who and what is best for you. If you feel that your choices are confusing, you will reach out to friends and family for help. But the only person who knows how you really feel is you. Listen up.

♣ *Three of Clubs* ♣

Mercury The writer's card. The story-teller's card. This can be one of the liar's cards, if surrounded by negative energies. Write, talk, communicate. Who do I call first? Lots of words, gabby-gus, lots on the mind, multiple emails (but double check it before you hit "reply all"). Studying multiple subjects, rewriting the book or proposal, having to make up your mind about something. Dealing with a learning disability.

Venus Writing or speaking to friends or family, lots of conversation, your message (or book) will be well received, the press is favorable, speak your mind.

Mars A passion for writing, speaking, teaching, communicating. Expressing yourself with gusto, charismatic speech and appearance. Multiple possibilities, ideas come fast and furious.

Jupiter Success as a writer or speaker, success can come from more than one place now, lots of travel brochures, deciding where to go from here.

Saturn Professional choices, a weighty or difficult decision. A challenging but valuable conversation with authority (your boss, your dad, etc). Too much on the mind, mental stress that impacts the health. Internet house hunting. Deadlines! Sort, file, prioritize, delegate, or trash it–but move the work off your desk!

Uranus Many sudden calls or interruptions. Sudden, spontaneous and serendipitous choices appear out of the blue. Unusual writing or communication, talking to foreigners, aliens, or just a weird group. Astrology really works! Invention, pretension, ascension. Can you really just fly away?

Neptune Visionary, intuitive ideas, courting the muse. (Too?) much psychic input, channeling many voices. Daydreaming, woolgathering, head in the clouds, both oars are not in the water.

Pluto Intensely pursuing a writing project, developing a deep well-spring of creativity. Decisions may seem weightier now, but you still make them one at a time, so put some thought into it. The power of choice and making up your own mind. Pushing through conversational barriers.

SUMMARY: The theme of the reading is choice, itself. It involves the thought process that governs our choices to begin with. This is the time for managing a variety of mental ideas all at once and/or channeling worry into productive creative output. Choosing none (or focusing on too many at once) may scatter your energies to the 4 winds. Select the most worthy ideas now for further development.

BIRTH CARD: If the 3 ♣ is your Birth Card, the art of rational decision making will be important to your life path. You will called upon to develop the mind and intellectual faculties, and you may have some important decisions to make which will require a clear head. At some point you may need to choose which of your many ideas to expand upon, and your choice may have far reaching consequences. In all intellectual matters, it will be important to listen to your head. But beware of fuzzy thinking or entertaining too many possibilities. If you become mentally frozen, you will make no decision at all, thereby abdicating your right to choose (and ultimately experiencing) what is best for you. If you feel that your choices are confusing, you will reach out to trusted colleagues or coworkers for help. But the only person who knows what you really think is you. Listen up.

♦ *Three of Diamonds* ♦

Mercury Exploring financial options, values changing over time—choices must reflect this, worry or indecision over finances, multiple bills, choosing who to pay, conflicting financial needs.

Venus Spending small amounts on home or family, considering changing your appearance in some way.

Mars Working multiple projects or jobs at the same time, aggressively pursuing a paycheck (or aggressively spending it), multiple opportunities, choosing the right job for right now.

Jupiter Creativity pays off, multiple income streams, happy financial decisions or deals, working some lucky breaks.

Saturn Multiple bills or debts, calculating opportunity costs (the cost of purchasing A is that, if you do, you may not also be able to purchase B). Making difficult budgetary decisions. Which house should you buy? Weigh all your options.

Uranus Several innovative money-making ideas at once. Unusual financial choices, a sudden expenditure (or spending spree). Shifting your financial priorities around, a sudden purchase to be made (or bill to be paid), deciding who gets what.

Neptune Financial intuition, "kid in a candy store" mentality, wishing for more. Get clear on what you value most. Choices can be confusing and the answer may not seem clear (or even rational) now, but follow your gut.

Pluto Becoming creative with your finances can be a transformational experience now, purchases must reflect a deeper system of values or you have wasted your money, the financial power of choice, deciding what to value. Pushing budgetary limits.

SUMMARY: The theme of the reading is the choice of what to value. This is a time when you will be dealing with financial decisions, or having multiple financial options and resources (which bill to pay, which job to take, which chair to buy, etc). Can also indicate multiple financial needs happening simultaneously. Opportunity cost must be factored into your decisions now.

BIRTH CARD: If the 3 ♦ is your Birth Card, financial decisions will play an important role in your life path. You will be called upon to develop your financial resources, and you may have important decisions to make that reflect your own personal value system. In all financial dealings, you must always be guided by your own values. But beware of becoming frozen, or of making no decision at all, thereby abdicating your right to choose (and ultimately experiencing) which values best suit you. If you feel that your choices are confusing, you will reach out to valued associates for help, but the only person who knows what you really value is you. Listen up.

♠ *Three of Spades* ♠

Mercury Multiple business calls, someone has to be on hold, multiple projects. An offer of work from several places at once, don't sweat it—just make your choice and move on.

Venus Working for friends or family may not be as simple as you thought, needing to service or please a variety of people all at once, mingling, networking, family demands.

Mars Energetically working multiple projects or jobs—try not to let it stress you out, just go with the flow. Choices regarding health or work matters. Deciding where (or with whom) your passions lie. Choosing where to best spend your available energy.

Jupiter "Spoilt for choice," successful multitasking, succeeding at several jobs at once, going in several directions at once, juggling it all and then some.

Saturn Working several projects or jobs at the same time can wear you down (or out), fatigue, being physically tired, needing to rest or take a break, poor health, being sick on the job, too pooped to pop. Taking the road less traveled might be better, but it's also a longer walk. Wear sturdy shoes.

Uranus Unexpected changes on the job or with health. Unusual work or health problems (as well as opportunities) require unconventional solutions. Think outside the box (or, for those of you who work for others it might be: "think outside the boss"). Focus, get organized. Otherwise expect to run around like a headless chicken.

Neptune Decisions, decisions, decisions. Your intuition works best now because your heart already knows the answer. Better living thru chemistry? Oh, just have a glass of wine and stop worrying so much! You'll live longer. Meditation may show you the way.

Pluto Too many cooks in the kitchen? Well, if it's too hot, get out. Finding a healthier way to "bring it" on the job, intensity works if it gets the job done, vigorous multitasking, channeling intensity into productive action, the physical (and metaphysical) power of choice. Pushing the job through.

SUMMARY: The theme of the reading is the choice of jobs. This is the time to deal with a variety of projects, jobs or health issues, and making decisions that will affect the future of your work and your overall health picture. The thing to remember is that you have the power of choice. Don't like the choice you made? Make another, and prepare to multitask.

BIRTH CARD: If the 3 ♠ is your Birth Card, career or health decisions will form a major part of your life path. At some point you may need to choose which job to focus on, or which project to select, and your choice may have far reaching consequences. In health matters, it will be important to listen to your body. Literally. But beware of vacillating between trying every new health fad that comes down the pike, and completely ignoring symptoms–making no decisions about health at all, thereby abdicating your right to choose (and ultimately experiencing) what might heal you and make you whole. If you feel that your choices are confusing, you will reach out to experts for help. But the only real expert on your body is you. Listen up.

Fours

The Fours are the "salt of the earth" people. They represent stability and grounding as well as marriage and the family unit as a whole. Fours have earned a stable enough foundation to be able to put down deep roots and nest. They are the ones most often content with the status quo. Yes, life is at a nicely balanced point with the Fours.

When you see Fours, think: "4-square" or box. Boxes are 4-sided and so are fences. While all this stability can help us to feel cozy and secure, we can also feel imprisoned at times in a cell of our own making. Sure, we're safe in there, but where's the adventure in that?

It's true, that sometimes the Four energy can be a bit too happy with things as they are, and too many Fours in a reading may indicate that the person has gotten themselves into a rut of sorts. A happy rut, no doubt, but a place of stasis, which is not always conducive to growth. Too much sameness can eventually lead to boredom. But "four" a time, at least, you have found your safe haven and all is well with the world!

 ♥ *Four of Hearts* ♥

Mercury A heart and mind in agreement, a proposal, love letters. Contentment with friends, good company.

Venus The marriage card. Strong family ties, nesting, happy homemaking, happiness in love, a beautiful and comfortable home. June Cleaver in "Leave it to Beaver" or "Happy Wife/Happy Life."

Mars Emotional energy available for family or friends, passion and drive when you need it, sexual fulfillment, satisfaction with the way things are right now.

Jupiter Expanding the family as planned (or not—it all goes to plan), family trip, traveling with loved ones (or a "stay-cation"), good times.

Saturn Karmic marriage or family ties, married to the job, family responsibilities, a solid citizen, a family man (or woman), working from home, building a solid home base, a loving foundation.

Uranus Family reunion, a happy elopement, a quick or sudden pairing, good surprises or positive (gentle) changes for the family unit. If you've suddenly realized you're stuck in a rut, you'll have support for making changes.

Neptune Dreaming of a happy family life, the perfect family picture, idyllic visions of how it should be, stability in your spiritual life.

Pluto A deep desire for love and family, wanting deep and lasting relationships. The power comes from stability; your family has transformed you.

SUMMARY: The theme of the reading is emotional stability and a peaceful heart. This is a time of happy, rewarding relationships. Your home is your nest, and you and your family are safe and warm and all snuggled in for the night. But, still, some may feel like their heart is in a rut, stuck in familiar people and feelings. The difference is this: are you sticking with them or are you stuck with them? The answer makes all the difference.

BIRTH CARD: If the 4 ♥ is your Birth Card, creating a loving family and building a stable home will be a major part of your path. The one danger here is that things may become so predictable that you may take the important people in your life for granted at times. So, every now and then, try to let the people you love know exactly how much they mean to you. And if it seems as though there isn't enough excitement or change in your life, try to cultivate a sense of gratitude for all that you do have (like love). OK, perhaps you don't live the life of a daredevil, but at least you're a home owner!

♣ *Four of Clubs* ♣

Mercury Stable communication, everyone feels heard and understood, a rational mind, well organized thoughts, practical ideas, the mind is calm and at peace.

Venus Stability at home, a solid foundation of family and friends, good communication with friends and loved ones, the conversation is all good.

Mars A passionate mind, intellectual ambitions, understanding the objectives makes the path easy to navigate. Walking your talk.

Jupiter Stability in life, good communications, learning is fun, lofty goals, solid travel plans, all connections are met with time to spare. Luck is with you, friends are everywhere.

Saturn The mind is strong and stable, organizing your thoughts, disciplining the mind for achievement and success, reliable communications on the job, "same old–same old" at the office, authority is predictable. A tendency to stubbornness, being stuck in a comfortable mental rut.

Uranus Sudden successful ideas, brilliant conversation, Steady progress with research or computer work. Surprising news from an old friend, someone suddenly reaches out and communicates. Spontaneous conversations go well.

Neptune Channeling spiritual information, dreaming of the solution, peaceful slumber, a perfect storm: the flow of ideas.

Pluto Deep intellectual contentment, good use of will, manifesting with the mind, thoughts become things.

SUMMARY: The theme of the reading is mental stability and peace of mind. At this time you can count on balanced perspectives, which lead to rational and intelligent conversation. Communication within the family flows smoothly now and friends are easy to talk to. But is your talk stuck in a comfortable groove? Conversation may benefit from new topics to stir things up once in a while.

BIRTH CARD: If the 4 ♣ is your Birth Card, educating the mind and cultivating excellent judgment will be a major part of your path. The one danger here is that the conversations in your life may become so routine that you may take it for granted that everyone values your opinion. So, every now and then, try to tell the people you communicate with that you also value what they have to say. You can do this best by listening respectfully. And if it sometimes seems as though there isn't enough excitement in your life or intellectual stimulation, try to cultivate a sense of gratitude for all that you do have (like friends). OK, perhaps you don't live the life of a daredevil, but at least your library is full!

♦ *Four of Diamonds* ♦

Mercury Money available for education or communication, a small monetary gift, the talk is about finance and value added.

Venus Money made in the home or money to spend on the home, improving ones appearance, buying art/gifts, shopping for comfort.

Mars Money to spend on hobbies or passions, knowing what's important looks good on you, putting your best foot forward.

Jupiter Financial stability, a lucky bet or investment, money to spend on travel or college, a solid education that leads to prosperous employment.

Saturn Traditional values, your work and financial life stabilize, learning to budget well in order to maintain financial balance, saving for a rainy day (or a house), a strong foundation.

Uranus Modern values, finances suddenly take a turn for the better, financial surprises that help you turn things around. Life is good again.

Neptune Stable spiritual values, money made thru psychic ability or intuition, metaphysical currency or cachet, hoping or dreaming of financial success and stability, donations to charity, supporting your cause, putting your money where your values lie, life—moving along swimmingly, a sound boat stays afloat.

Pluto Becoming clear about what you personally value takes the drama out of your financial situation, getting to the bottom of your fear of prosperity (or the fear of handling your own money), overcoming a poverty consciousness, a financial crisis passes. Stabilizing your finances makes life less intense and gives you some peace. You do what you can, then release the rest.

SUMMARY: The theme of the reading is financial stability. This is a time to shore up your holdings and enjoy some stability. Your values have created a solid foundation to build upon. You will likely enjoy the success you have earned now, as finances proceed on an even keel in your life. But if you're bored with all this, look to see where else you can create added value.

BIRTH CARD: If the 4 ♦ is your Birth Card, creating security and a solid sense of values will be a major part of your path. The one danger here is that the money in your professional life may be so good that you may allow it to trap you in a position that requires no real effort on your part. And you may end up taking your coworkers or teammates for granted So, every now and then, try to let your them know that you also value their contributions to the team or the company. You can do this best by sharing the credit for a job well done. And if it sometimes seems as though there isn't enough excitement in your life or variety in your daily routine, try to cultivate a sense of gratitude for all that you do have (like security). OK, perhaps you don't live the life of a daredevil, but at least you've got a retirement fund!

♠ Four of Spades ♠

Mercury A calm and peaceful mind, communication at work is satisfying, compromises are reached, messages regarding health bring resolution or good news, situations are stable.

Venus Home life is solid. Successfully working from home or on the home, female bosses love you, successful work projects, health is stable, beauty shines from the inside out, becoming fit, creating good health and work habits.

Mars Successful work projects, male bosses love you, energy is stable, health is good, working out, improving one's physique.

Jupiter Good fortune at work, success with coworkers, employees, and higher ups, things work out.

Saturn Stabilizing your health and creating health routines that improve how you feel, balance in your work life, enjoying a solid foundation overall.

Uranus For once, the surprises on the job are all good ones, Internet and computer work is favorable, your health takes a turn for the better. Suddenly realizing how good you got it!

Neptune Psychic or metaphysical work is successful, creating balance, health evens out. The signs are clear, the message received, your dreams are perfectly content now. For once you might even get to sleep in!

Pluto Challenging yourself to make your home and work life more stable. Creating balance now can transform your whole life. The secrets are all safe. Everything is secure and locked up tight.

SUMMARY: The theme of the reading is stability with health and work. At this time you can create and enjoy a truly balanced life. Your career has entered a very safe phase and you are happy with the job you landed. "God's in His heaven and all's right with the world." Never satisfied? Then explore what other ladders you might climb.

BIRTH CARD: If the 4 ♠ is your Birth Card, creating a solid, stable life that satisfies you will be a major part of your path in some way. The one danger here is that life in general may simply become too predictable and you may take it for granted that everything will always just fall magically into place. Or, you may simply fail to feel satisfied, despite your many blessings, and indulge in self-pity. So, every now and then, look around and really see all the blessings that life has given you. You can do this best by noticing how many people don't have it as good or as easy as you do. And if it sometimes seems as though there isn't enough excitement in your life or your purpose doesn't seem challenging enough, try to cultivate a sense of gratitude for all that you do have (like your job). OK, perhaps you don't live the life of a daredevil, but at least you've got your health!

Fives

♥ ♣ ♦ ♠ ♥ ♣ ♦ ♠

Unlike the Fours, which promote staying put, the Fives are ever in motion and promote change. They represent movement in one's affairs. Of course, that movement is not always guaranteed to be in the right direction, but at least you're not standing still any more!

The Five has many types of motion and one of them is travel. Five can indicate a single important trip, an extended period of traveling, or in some cases, actual relocation. However long you're away from home, once you're free to move about the country, you are also free to have an adventure (another side of the Five). A different kind of Five movement involves changing partners. For some this may seem scarier than traveling, but sometimes in life change is necessary for growth.

So remember, the Five is a mover and a shaker. If life has become stuck or stagnant at all, you can count on Five energy to get things moving again!

Mercury A change of heart, fickleness, perhaps not knowing what you want? Giving love away, flitting here and there, "gadding" about, gossip, many invitations, many conversations.

Venus A separation, a heart divided, changeable affections, a change of heart, changes within the home or family, moving out, socially busy, a change of social plans, a change in friends, "girls just wanna have fun" (they just wanna).

Mars An emotional issue quickly resolved, energetic groups of people coming and going, unstable or changeable emotional state, dissipated affections, boys just "wanna have fun" too (and they usually do).

Jupiter Road trip, learning or traveling with friends, a variety of people and amusements, taking the road less traveled, going off-map/off-site, changing travel companions.

Saturn Lovesick, emotions have you stressed out, a difficult separation, a changing of the guard, not feeling the love anymore for your job, needing a new career path.

Uranus A sudden change of heart, a spontaneous trip, serendipity, meeting unusual and interesting people along the way, dealing with changeable, unstable, or moody people.

Neptune Hanging out with musical and artistic types, highly intuitive or creative friends. Your vision changes, a new spiritual path, the spirit moves you.

Pluto Challenges or encounters with intense people, a dramatic change of heart, a heart in transition, deeply emotional and personal changes, knowing your own heart first is the key to everything else.

SUMMARY: The theme of the reading is emotional change. You are having a change of heart about someone or something and it may be time to change up who you know. Your emotions are in transition now and will need extra time and freedom to process. Have your friends or acquaintances been holding you back? You are the company you keep and perhaps you need a changing of the guard. Open yourself up to new companions in life.

BIRTH CARD: If the 5 ♥ is your Birth Card, a change of heart will be a major part of your life in some way. Your emotions are changeable and versatile and you are meant to have a variety of experiences in love and relationships in order to discover who and what you need most. You are exploring love in all its splendor, and this includes friends as well as lovers and other partners. Because your primary relationships may vary, it may take you to parts unknown, and travel may also be a part of your road to love and family. You are likely to keep your options open so you can be ready at a moment's notice for the "the one" you seek. But along the way, you may find the destination is not nearly as interesting as the journey.

♣ Five of Clubs ♣

Mercury Restless thoughts, changing your mind, not knowing what to think, changing the subject, changing your plans, a big "to-do" list, words in motion.

Venus Changing partners or friends, a change of scenery, rearranging the furniture or reorganizing your home.

Mars Mental and physical restlessness, switching gears, needing a change from routine. It's time to put the book (phone, i pad, whatever) down and take a walk outside.

Jupiter The "armchair traveler." The mind goes on its own little adventure, reading or researching new or far-off places or topics, a change of travel plans, changing your major, a change of venue, planning the trip.

Saturn Making difficult changes to your plans, staying flexible. Changes require extra effort. Try to de-stress and protect your health.

Uranus An unplanned, last-minute or spontaneous trip, a move or change of scene. Throw out the itinerary and wing it, an open mind expands your horizons. An unexpected conversation.

Neptune Changes to your spiritual beliefs or ideals. Try a different approach, the dream changes everything, Plotting a course through foggy seas. When you think one thing but feel another, listen to your gut.

Pluto A challenge to your ideas or plans, a mind (or specific thought process) in transition. Changing your mind can change your life, you are who and what you think you are.

SUMMARY: The theme of the reading is intellectual change. You are changing your mind about something or someone and it may be time to make a new plan. Your ideas are in transition now, and you need time to think. Avoid worrying, it won't change the outcome. Focus instead on positive thoughts. Allow room for the "impossible." Open your mind to new concepts, new beliefs, or new paradigms and embrace courageous new ideas. Now is the time to change what it is you think you know. The winds of change may be inevitable, but you'll be happiest if you get to be the one to decide which way the wind will blow.

BIRTH CARD: If the 5 ♣ is your Birth Card, a change of mind will be a major part of your life in some way. Your thoughts and ideas are changeable and in transition and you are meant to have a multitude of opinions on things. But what you think will not always match how you feel and you are meant to experience the disconnect between the mind and heart so that you can explore the best way to unite them. Your educational path may take you through several schools of thought (literally or not). Progressing from one teacher to the next may take you to parts unknown, and travel may also be a part of your road to the knowledge you seek. Your ideas may change with each shiny new textbook, but along the way you may find that the destination is not nearly as interesting as the journey.

Mercury A change in financial goals, creating a budget, changing your mind about what you value or want, a "quick-change" artist. A quick purchase or making a fast buck.

Venus Money going out, spending on changes made to the home, a shopping trip, a new you, a makeover. Paying the rent or mortgage, a change in payments, money owed to women.

Mars Aggressive spending, money going out as fast as it comes in (or faster!), debt collectors. Changing your hobbies or passions.

Jupiter Pricing the trip or the move, or, not going because you can't afford it, money going out, spending (or overspending) on travel or education, being overcharged, trying to keep up with growing expenses, charity, generosity, giving until it hurts.

Saturn Difficult financial changes related to your work or business, cutbacks, layoffs, downsizing, a change of job. Positive cash flow may be slow in coming. The sale of a home or property.

Uranus Unexpected financial changes, forgotten bills, expenses suddenly rise, money going out. The sudden realization that you're worth more than you're paid.

Neptune A change in finances may come from wishing for a change, following your intuition may change your direction, strive for financial clarity now, be clear on what you value.

Pluto A transformational change in circumstances. Let go of what can't be controlled. Finances in transition. Changing where or how you make your living. Deeply held beliefs about prosperity must be uncovered. Release poverty, allow prosperity in equal measure.

SUMMARY: The theme of the reading is financial change. This is a time when you will consider making changes to how you make your living. Your values are shifting and changing now, and you'll need to reorder your priorities in order to maximize your full potential. Your expenses may be shifting and changing as well, and no matter which changes you decide on, some money must be spent. But it's how you actually view the material side of life as a whole that is really in transition. Open yourself to the possibilities of a new career path. Change is inevitable at this time, and you'll be happiest if you're the one to decide which way it goes.

BIRTH CARD: If the 5 ♦ is your Birth Card, a change in values will be a major part of your life in some way. What has meaning for you is changing and shifting, as your values expand, and you are meant to experience the difference between having values and living by them. Your finances may also fluctuate from time to time, and learning the best way to pay the bills may be a work in progress, as you try out multiple jobs or explore different professions. Because your career path may vary, it may take you to parts unknown, and travel may also be a part of your road to security. You are likely to keep your assets liquid and ready at a moment's notice for the next big financial opportunity. But along the way you may find that the destination is not nearly as interesting as the journey.

♠ *Five of Spades* ♠

Mercury A change of job, on-the-job training, learning by doing. Changing your position, the need to renegotiate agreements. Talking about health, changes to your daily routine, a doctor's appointment is canceled or changed.

Venus Relocation, a change in residence, people moving in and out. A change in personnel. Does no one just stay put anymore?

Mars Moving, a change of residence, travel. Changes in physical condition, a new diet or exercise regimen that can improve health and restore energy levels ("hot" yoga?).

Jupiter A fortunate change in location, a welcome change of plans or scenery, your studies take you in a different direction, successful travel, "the Force is with you." A refreshing change of pace.

Saturn A move or relocation, property changing hands. Changes at work or with health. Challenges now will highlight where you need to make changes. Movement in work projects, a meeting is changed or canceled.

Uranus A long-distance trip, flying, strange new lands, a sudden move, plans that change dramatically, sudden health changes.

Neptune A long trip over water, a vacation, sacred travel, a spiritual journey or pilgrimage. Water therapies improve health.

Pluto Moving can either be challenging or transformational—your attitude makes all the difference, a life or career in transition, your work enters a new phase, you change paths.

SUMMARY: The theme of the reading is CHANGE, period! This is an action-oriented card so anything and everything is subject to change now: including travel, your health, where you live, the route you take to work, what you do for a living, etc. Many people do take trips or decide to relocate with this card. This also indicates that it might be a good time to change your over all health and how you approach your own wellbeing. Whether it's diet or stress, making changes to your daily routine can improve things. So which is it for you? Do you need to improve your health, relocate, accept a new job, tackle a new project? Or is it "all of the above?" Your entire life is in transition now and changes will be plentiful. Shake things up, take a chance, and open yourself up to a whole new way of life.

BIRTH CARD: If the 5 ♠ is your Birth Card, a change of destiny will be a major part of your life in some way. Your purpose is in transition and you are meant to have a variety of soul-searching expeditions to find your place in the world. Your health may also fluctuate from time to time, and taking care of yourself may be a work in progress, as you try first this remedy and then that one. Because your destiny may take you to parts unknown, travel may also be a major part of your trip to self-discovery, or you may relocate in order to pursue your chosen path. Bags packed and ready at a moment's notice to hit the open road, you may find that the destination is not nearly as interesting as the journey.

Sixes

♥ ♣ ♦ ♠ ♥ ♣ ♦ ♠

Some writers on the card system have noted that Sixes seem "boring" or "routine." Nothing could be further from the truth. The Sixes represent karma, retribution, forgiveness and–ultimately–balance. All Sixes seek to balance the books and that is where karma enters into it: both karma accrued and karma dissolved. For what you have sown, you reap. Because this can be true physically (as well as metaphysically), the Sixes sometimes have messages for us regarding our overall health status, especially in the Spades suit.

When we fail to process their lessons, all Sixes can sometimes promote delays and keep us feeling stuck, but–and you'll just have to trust me here–this does not equate to boredom!

When handled wisely, Sixes can also promote peace and acceptance. After all, there is a kind of peace to knowing you've done all you can do. There is grace in the quiet acceptance of what cannot be changed.

All Sixes have "deliverance" as part of their overall mission statement. And for many of them, "delivering" will be literal. By sharing what they know, they dissolve karma and achieve a peaceful stasis. And they remind us to stick with what we already know, to use what we already have. They bring home the lesson that there can be no balance without patience, that there is a time to act and a time to lay low.

When reading a Six ask yourself if all that could be done/given has been. If it has, then just let it be and stay where you are for now. Think of it like life's little placeholder or as a temporary Stop sign. Because there are times in life when doing nothing (at least for the moment) is the right move. Remember though, that when waters appear to be still, there can still be quite a tidal wave of activity just beneath the surface. Sixes are tricky that way. Don't underestimate them!

♥ *Six of Hearts* ♥

Mercury Relationships require compromise and mature communication now, giving or getting a heart-felt apology works wonders.

Venus Fulfilling your social obligations, plans canceled, a long-term relationship, karmic love or karma with loved ones, heartsick, balancing your emotions and home life. Stick with who you already know. Practice random acts of kindness (to yourself as well as others).

Mars Karmic passions/sexual partners, past life lovers, learning the value of patience, balancing your passions. Your love life may seem boring or on hold now. Slow and steady wins the race.

Jupiter Good love karma returns to you now, a friend returns a favor. Unpack your bags because you're better off staying put, and friends will come to you. A well-balanced education benefits all, being well informed. A humorous approach works best now.

Saturn Holding your own, relationship karma will require maturity, being responsible for (or to) family or friends, coworkers may seem more like family now, a balanced (or boring) work life.

Uranus Spontaneous group meetings, "save the date," fulfilling your promises to the team, humanitarian groups, reaching a tipping point.

Neptune Sacrifices made for a friend (or friends make sacrifices for you), spiritual karma with friends or family, psychic insights into loved ones, a dream temporarily on hold, the eyes, no change in vision or "the sight," a balanced perspective or stuck in a spiritual rut. Living a spiritual life requires true spiritual principles.

Pluto Taking responsibility for your relationship issues dissolves karma, getting back what you give in relationships (or what you deserve). Owning your personal power and how you use it.

Sixes 99

SUMMARY: The theme of the reading is love and relationship karma as we balance out what we do for love (or loved ones). Relationships are a two-way street. Other people can act as mirrors now (or you can act as mirror for them) to show you how you really feel. Let your heart be still—let it rest and heal. Simple kindness is important now—both given and received. At this time you attract into your life the people you think you deserve. Do you deserve better? The best!

BIRTH CARD: If the 6 ♥ is your Birth Card, you are dealing with balancing out the karma of relationships. Relating to others in a responsible manner is your most important focus in this lifetime, and you must stay true to your love. You will always feel your connection with others (whether positive or negative) acutely. And you may even go into one of the counseling professions. But whether you are working with many other people's families or just your own little family, your duty this time around is to assist others to relate. *Deliver the Love!*

♣ *Six of Clubs* ♣

Mercury Think well before speaking. Speak your truth and keep your word. Internal processing. Writing and research may be stalled, writer's block. Intellectual compromise, setting the record straight, balanced thoughts=balanced speech. On the other hand, no news is good news.

Venus Honoring your social commitments, promises made/promises kept, being true to you, no change at home or with family. Your proposal goes unanswered for the moment. Staying home, canceling plans.

Mars Walking your talk (literally), developing your ambitious ideas requires patience not muscle, work smarter not harder. Putting "mental muscle" into dissolving karma can help. But "if it ain't broke, don't fix it!"

Jupiter Good communication karma returns to you now, ideas flow, the talk about you is all good, a sound mind, a balanced intellect. Travel to help someone in need, a karmic trip or delayed travel plans. But the delay is in your favor now.

Saturn Fulfilling your obligations now may be hard, but it will lead to a peaceful mind, knowing that you did your best, sticking to your guns. Taking full responsibility for your ideas.

Uranus Speaking up when others can't, defending the right to free speech, having your say, regardless of the cost.

Neptune Highly intuitive, a psychic mind, the medium, channeled messages, stable sight, recording what you see for posterity.

Pluto Taking responsibility for your words and the way in which you use them. Dissolving the karma of intentions, purifying your thoughts.

SUMMARY: The theme of the reading is truth and being true to your word; meaning what you say, saying what you mean. All things begin with an idea. Form yours carefully and thoughtfully now. Walk your talk.

BIRTH CARD: If the 6 ♣ is your Birth Card, you are dealing with balancing out the karma of information. Responsible communication is your most important focus in this lifetime and you must stay true to your word. Your intuition is very strong, and you may even be a psychic or medium. This connection to the spirit world can guide you, and as with all gifts, it is meant to be given away. But whether you are channeling angelic prophecies or esoteric knowledge, your duty this time around is to make the information available to seekers everywhere. *Deliver the Message!*

♦ *Six of Diamonds* ♦

Mercury Discussing the bills, agreements around repayment of debts. Effective cost-cutting measures may require time to produce results. Patience is required in all communication.

Venus Paying off a home (or expenses related to the home), repaying family debts, organizing the bills, a karmic home. Refurbish/re-purpose what you already possess rather than buying new.

Mars Energy is best used to finish up what you have already started, use what you already have, waste not/want not. Delay unnecessary spending. Quickly and aggressively dissolving financial karma.

Jupiter Good money karma returns to you and debts can now be collected, college scholarships, money available for travel, money made from teaching.

Saturn Paying off heavy debts, saving for the future, long-term bills, paying over time, balancing the books, money karma. Stick with the clients you already have and finish the work already paid for.

Uranus A forgotten bill, sudden or unplanned expenses, diverting funds to pay off debts, yard sale, financial donations or gifts. Suddenly releasing money karma.

Neptune All that glitters is not gold, dreams may be costly now, so save up (because we all need our dreams), spiritual karma regarding value and self-worth.

Pluto Repayment of debt (to you or by you), dissolving financial karma, dealing with a scarcity mentality, fairness and honesty in all interactions will dissolve karma.

SUMMARY: The theme of the reading is financial karma or results, financial responsibility, balancing your books. You should not live in the red, but neither is a life lived in the black any better unless you understand the karmic law of prosperity. Allow prosperity to flow freely—both from you and to you. One can only give or receive with an open hand.

BIRTH CARD: If the 6 ♦ is your Birth Card, you are dealing with balancing out the karma of prosperity. Gainful employment and the proper use of your resources is your most important focus in this lifetime, and you must stay true to your values. Whatever profession you choose, you must balance your checkbook (literally), and you must avoid debt. But you must first and foremost possess a balanced system of personal core values. And, in the true spirit of generosity, some of what you make must be shared or given away. *Deliver Abundance!*

♠ *Six of Spades* ♠

Mercury Communication at work may require extra effort, keep proprietary data private, keep secrets to yourself, don't gossip, loose lips sink ships, headaches (literal or figurative), sinus trouble, getting your head on straight. Health needs more effort.

Venus Working from home or with family presents its own problems now, but it may be better to stay home and work. Attention to your diet and lifestyle will improve health, female reproductive health. Plans stall and may be postponed or canceled altogether.

Mars Energy may be lower than usual now, safeguard your health, know your own limits and don't push yourself physically. Take a reduced schedule, you need time to retreat and regroup. Male reproductive health.

Jupiter Good work karma returns to you now, important information finds you just when you need it. There is wisdom in staying the course now.

Saturn Physical exhaustion. Calling in sick. Pace yourself at work, complete work already begun rather than beginning something new. Instead of soliciting new clients, service the ones you already have. In business you get what you deserve now, if you did the work, you get the paycheck. May also indicate unemployment. See the dentist.

Uranus Sudden or unexpected jobs that need to be handled carefully or fixed/redone quickly, yet you may not have everything you need to do the job. News or insight about your health, a sudden illness may sideline you temporarily. Things progress in fits and starts, stop/go energies. Rest in-between things.

Neptune Sleeping more, doing less because you need the rest, canceling your plans, no activity, downtime, convalescence, prophetic dreams or visions. Medical tests may be delayed or the results may be confusing. Sometimes doing nothing is exactly what is needed. Being still and peaceful, seeing rest as the cure.

Pluto Taking full responsibility for work and health choices dissolves karma, balancing diet, exercise and lifestyle choices improves both your present and your future. Your workload may be tedious for the time being, but complaining intensely about it can only make it worse. Exhaustion!

SUMMARY: The theme of the reading is health and work karma, and your ability (or willingness) to maintain the status quo. At this time you should be focused on finishing what's already started as opposed to beginning new things, adding more jobs, taking on additional projects, etc. This is not the time to chase health fads or quick fixes. Your health will be best served now by following regular, daily health routines, and by improving the things you do each day that will support future health. This card represents the sum total of our behavior towards ourselves and our personal lifestyle choices. Ask yourself: Do you eat well or poorly? Do you work at something you love or hate? Are you a workaholic? Actions have consequences. Your body and mind are connected. Treat them well and they will repay the favor.

BIRTH CARD: If the 6 ♠ is your Birth Card, you are dealing with balancing out the karma of work and service. Finding a purpose worthy of you is your most important focus in this lifetime, and once found, you must stay true to your purpose. Because of this, you may have greater choice than some of the other Sixes. You will also need to balance out your health with right and careful living. But whether you are working in a soup kitchen or the head of your own gym, your duty this time around is to honor your divine purpose by assisting others in your own special way. *Whatever you Deliver–Deliver it Selflessly.*

Sevens

♥ ♣ ♦ ♠ ♥ ♣ ♦ ♠

The Sevens represent the great spiritual rewards that can be ours if we can overcome the challenges and obstacles associated with this magical number. When we have learned the lessons that Seven has to teach us (and some of them are quite challenging), we can then transcend the pitfalls associated with them and access the true blessings within.

If the challenges are very difficult, then the Seven card may indicate periods of depression, trials and tribulations, and/or sacrifices that must be made for others. It's interesting to note that both the Sixes and

Sevens may attract past life people into their lives in order to complete some unfinished lessons and balance their karmic books.

If your reading contains many Sevens, that may indicate a challenging time. The trick with Sevens is to learn to "rise above" or transcend mundane concerns and to release personal expectations or attachments to the outcome. But rising above often requires some personal sacrifice. This makes the Seven both one of the most difficult and one of the most blessed cards in the deck.

♥ *Seven of Hearts* ♥

Mercury Challenges and/or blessings in communicating in a loving manner. Challenged to control your emotions, so that they, in turn, don't control your mind. Having a difficult "heart to heart" talk. Release your expectations and the talks will eventually improve.

Venus Challenges and/or blessings with the women in your life, or in marriage and important relationships, rising above personal attachment in love and allowing your partner to be the best possible version of themselves, personal sacrifices made for the family.

Mars Challenges and/or blessings with the men in your life, feeling lost or confused in relationships, problems expressing yourself sexually, personal attractions may prove challenging (you may be attracted to someone who's not currently available), meeting the challenge of developing healthy relationship patterns.

Jupiter Challenges and/or blessings in traveling to or visiting with friends and family (the challenge may be with the trip itself or with various family members).

Saturn Challenges and/or blessings at work, the sacrifices one must make in relationships, releasing personal attachment or expectation, a challenge to authority, problems with employees must be worked out delicately but with authority.

Uranus Challenges and/or blessings in expressing universal or impersonal love. Caring for those who cannot care for themselves.

Neptune Challenges and/or blessings in expressing spiritual love ("let go, let God"), releasing or forgiving people, hearing your angels sing. Mystical work, compassion and kindness make a difference always!

Pluto Challenged to love unconditionally (and to allow yourself to be loved unconditionally), loving without attachment or judgment. Dealing with fears of abandonment (yours or a loved one's), love can transform you. When walking with spirit we never walk alone.

SUMMARY: The theme of the reading is emotional catharsis and the trials associated with it. You are letting go of what you "want" to be, and allowing what "needs" to be. You may be called upon to sacrifice your needs for the good of another, realizing that sometimes the highest love is spiritual–and without personal attachment. In purging your emotional past, you are learning to release personal expectation and to trust in the love that comes. And though you cannot rush it, it comes at just the right time.

BIRTH CARD: If the 7 ♥ is your Birth Card, your blessings and challenges alike will come through your interactions with others. This card requires selfless service and dedication in all your relationships, but without the expectation of personal reward. In all relationships, you will be required to purge any part of your nature that is possessive or jealous. You will do well if you can rise above self-pity and a tendency to dwell on your personal disappointments. Responsibilities to others must be met with a strong heart and not avoided; and for you, love must be spiritual, universal and freely given. Once you gain entry to the right group of people, you will be blessed with a true sense of community and a peaceful heart. Larger group interaction or service, especially those with a humanitarian cause, may be very rewarding and within that group you may know success.

Mercury Challenges and/or blessings in communicating effectively, learning to listen as well as talk, changing negative self-talk into pep talk.

Venus Sacrifices made for loved ones, challenged by negative attitudes towards family and friends, dissatisfaction with your home/family or choosing to live in the heart of wisdom, knowing your own heart and mind, releasing expectations of others frees both of you.

Mars Challenged by negative attitudes or feelings towards life or others, arguing, debating. Thinking positively can improve your energy level.

Jupiter Challenges and/or blessings with travel, vacation, or educational plans. The messages from far away may be uncertain or you may find it challenging to see the big picture. Looking on the bright side may be difficult now, but every cloud does, indeed, have a silver lining. Look harder (and farther).

Saturn Challenges and/or blessings with mental projects at work. You are challenged now to think positively, but a positive attitude will help you to work thru issues or solve problems one at a time. Having to be the grown-up, a teachable moment. Consulting physician, a second opinion.

Uranus A sudden challenge appears to change your thought process, think it over, change your mind. It might be the blessing you were looking for.

Neptune Challenges and/or blessings with spiritual beliefs, vague indistinct worry, free-floating anxiety. Unplug and Keep the Faith!

Pluto Challenged to develop a truly enlightened mind, dark thoughts. Controlling personal negativity transforms both you and the situation, learning self-control, rising above.

SUMMARY: The theme of the reading is intellectual catharsis and the trials that go along with it. This is a time of seeing the effects of negative speech patterns (your own or another's). You are learning to rise above personal attachment to how you think about things, and also to let go of any preconceived ideas or expectations around important conversations and agreements. By purging your mind of negative thoughts and fears, you are able to release personal expectation, and to trust the information that comes. Once you have composed the right message, trust that it will be delivered–at the right moment in time.

BIRTH CARD: If the 7 ♣ is your Birth Card, your blessings and trials alike will come through all communication efforts. This card requires selfless service and dedication, especially in a mental capacity, but without the normal expectation of personal reward. For instance, you may be required to give freely of your ideas, and some of them may greatly benefit others. You will do well if you can rise above the tendency to complain, worry excessively, or to scatter your thoughts. Responsible communication comes from a strong, well-disciplined mind, and is a must. Once you find the correct path to knowledge, you will be blessed with a true sense of accomplishment and a tranquil mind. Institutions of higher learning or research, especially those allowing you to combine your strong intellect and ideas with others, may be very rewarding and within those "hallowed walls" you may know success.

✦ *Seven of Diamonds* ✦

Mercury Challenges and/or blessings with business communication, having to walk your talk, talking about the budget and how to improve it. Giving more than you get.

Venus Challenges and/or blessings in finances, money spent on family, live in the heart of that which you most cherish, count your blessings.

Mars Challenges and/or blessings with overly aggressive spending. Money flows out and quickly. Make sure it's going where it needs to.

Jupiter Are you Rich or Poor? Whatever your answer is, you're right. Challenges and/or blessings in appreciating true prosperity and abundance, making deposits in the goodwill bank. Purging the poverty consciousness or scarcity mindset that keeps you trapped.

Saturn Challenges and/or blessings at work, worrying about losing your job, keep your head down and just do your job now, handling a tricky situation with experience and maturity. Paying the doctor bills.

Uranus Financial challenges and/or blessings that come up suddenly or unexpectedly, but you can rise above them just as quickly.

Neptune Wishing for prosperity. Allow beauty to help you rise above it (music, art, poetry). Many worthwhile things in life are already free.

Pluto Challenges or blessings (or both) with resources. Transforming a poverty consciousness into an abundance mentality, dealing with the possibility of bankruptcy. Perhaps bankruptcy will allow you to begin again, but is it really your only (or best) choice? Choose carefully, your value system can transform your life now.

SUMMARY: The theme of the reading is financial catharsis and the trials associated with it. This is a time of releasing old or outworn values or things that no longer serve your highest good. True wealth follows an attitude of gratitude. You are learning to rise above materialism and personal attachment to things, trusting that a higher value will remain. The trick is to be able to see (and value) what you already have, not to pine after what you don't. Those who appreciate what they have are already wealthy. Those who can't, never will be.

BIRTH CARD: If the 7 ♦ is your Birth Card, your blessings and challenges alike will come through your financial dealings and affairs. Whether you inherit it, marry it, or work for it yourself, the state of your resources plays an important part in your life. And this will be true whether there is poverty or wealth. But it is your own personal value system that will determine your happiness. This card requires selfless service and a true spirit of generosity, but without the normal expectation of personal reward. For instance, you may be required to give freely of your time and resources to benefit others (your talents and abilities are also resources). And you may not even get a "thank-you" for your trouble! Do it anyway. You will do well if you can rise above the tendency to gamble, keep score or to fritter away your resources. Workaholics or working just for the paycheck should also be avoided. Being financially responsible comes from a solid, well-developed set of core values, and is a must. Once you find the correct path to security, you will be blessed with a balanced ledger—both physically and metaphysically. But it's knowing your own true worth that ultimately brings you peace. Philanthropic institutions or non-profit groups offer opportunities to "put your money where your mouth is" and within them you may know success.

♠ *Seven of Spades* ♠

Mercury Challenges and/or blessings in communicating on the job. When yelling has no impact, just whisper. The office gossip may be especially negative now. Rise above and pay it no mind.

Venus Challenges and/or blessings in working partnerships, getting things done at home now may be difficult—keep at it, live in the moment. Health challenges or problems with women in the home, female trouble.

Mars Challenges and/or blessings with sexual expression or in finding your real passion. Fighting, curbing the appetites, health challenges, problems with men, challenged to find an appropriate way to express anger. Improving the health requires energy and consistent effort, male trouble.

Jupiter Challenges and/or blessings in travel for work, learning difficult lessons on the job, not enjoying the seminar—stick with it. Climbing a mountain is accomplished by taking one step up at a time.

Saturn Challenges and/or blessings at work or in overcoming negative patterning in health and work, changing bad habits, the consequences of previous actions. Seeing the doc.

Uranus Challenges and/or blessings in accepting that which you cannot change, having no attachment to the outcome, acceptance. A health or work challenge comes up unexpectedly.

Neptune Challenges and/or blessings in expressing one's true spirit, unshakable faith in all things (or the complete lack of faith). Something to ponder: On the bus of life, you don't always have to be the driver. Sometimes the passengers have the best view!

Pluto Challenges and/or blessings in creating good habits for health, well-being, or work; balancing work and health transforms your whole life. The difference between having beliefs and living them. Walking your talk, living your faith even thru the dark night of the soul, knowing that the truth will set you free.

SUMMARY: The theme of the reading is physical catharsis and the trials associated with it. This is a time of releasing health patterns or bad habits that no longer serve your highest good. You are learning to rise above physical addictions, trusting in a higher power to guide you through. You may also be letting go of empty jobs that drain you, or seeing for the first time where your efforts really belong. Once you recognize the right path for you, trust that your time walking that path will be well spent.

BIRTH CARD: If the 7 ♠ is your Birth Card, your blessings and trials alike will come through work and health-related issues. This is a card of selfless service to others and will require you to rise above personal needs so that you can meet the needs of others, but without the normal expectation of personal rewards. For instance, you may be required to donate your time to complete other people's projects, or to lend your physical stamina in some way, which may help them. You will do well if you can rise above the tendency toward poor or irregular health habits. A tendency towards chronic restlessness should also be avoided, as the body needs rest as well as exercise. Acting on a strong sense of purpose is only possible for you if you maintain a healthy body and so having a good health regimen is a must for you. Once found, a true sense of divine purpose will bless you with health in both body and soul. You have true sight at your disposal, if you will but use it, and you see what is hidden from others. Once you have learned to trust your inner guidance and intuitive wisdom, you may know success.

The Eights represent power and contain the strongest protection possible from any type of obstacle, including illness. With the strength of the Eight, you can vault over all obstacles in your path and overcome all challenges (or challengers).

It's like having a giant energy shield all around you, protecting you on all fronts. When I find myself in a questionable situation (or with dubious people) I literally picture an "8" in my mind and think "Shields UP!." I instantly feel surrounded by a protective light. Try it yourself.

And then, of course, there's the "Magic 8-Ball" – that mysterious "all seeing" oracle that we all consulted as kids when we really needed to know the answer to something! Don't lie, I know that at least some of you still have them. Eights are powerful, but the power needs to be used for good.

If you see Eights in a reading, know that there is protection available and that the person being read for can choose to apply their strong will to whatever situation they find themselves in, or to manifest whatever it is that they need. Notice that the "8" is shaped like the infinity symbol and represents the never ending circle of life. It holds the promise that we are eternal. This number is something of a Magician or Spiritual Warrior. And you hold the power.

♥ Eight of Hearts ♥

Mercury Overcoming all challenges in communication with love, speaking your heart, overcoming (and healing from) personal disappointment. Love flows to you and from you through words, happy news about loved ones.

Venus Protection for your heart (literally, your heart is healthy) and over all loved ones, family reunion, warm feelings all around. A socially fulfilling time.

Mars Protection in love and competition, challenging other suitors and winning, "getting the girl" (or guy). Someone loves you fiercely and with all their heart.

Jupiter Travel with friends and family (or visiting friends and family), protection, being in good company, being able to safely expand your circle of friends now.

Saturn A heart protected, overcoming all problems at work (or with co-workers), surmounting problems in relationships through hard work. Time has healed the wound.

Uranus Others help you succeed now, sudden or unexpected success with the public. Your "boo" has your back.

Neptune Protection in love and in relationships, divine intervention, angels surround you, ask for help or divine guidance and it will be there.

Pluto The power of love transforms your life, protection in personal relationships, transforming disappointment with love, intense personal transformation.

SUMMARY: The theme of the reading is protection for all your important relationships. When love goes well, relationships thrive. The people you care for are loved and protected. There may be gatherings of friends or family reunions now, along with a period of social enrichment.

BIRTH CARD: If the 8 ♥ is your Birth Card, yours is the power of people. Developing a healthy relationship style with the people most important to you, will be a major part of your life. Dealing with people in positions of power (or being one yourself) allows you to enjoy a protected life. And because you give all you have, you must never work in a field that doesn't suit you. In the personal arena "to love and be loved in return" is your goal. When your love life works, everything else seems golden. But when you struggle for control within your relationships, everything falls apart. Part of the problem may be your high expectations in love; we are none of us perfect. Also, never at a loss for company, you might perhaps be better off spending more time with the one who means the most. Your strong will combined with a loving approach, will bring happiness and success both personally and professionally. Personal relationships will always benefit most from personal attention.

♣ *Eight of Clubs* ♣

Mercury Mind Power. Picturing the best possible outcome. Protection for your original ideas, your identity and documents are secure. Speaking or writing well, the phone call goes through, the connections are made, good news travels fast.

Venus Successful social activity, overcoming all obstacles at home or with family members, your circle of friends is protected.

Mars Passionately pursuing your goals brings success, spreading your ideas, speaking with passion and conviction, overcoming anger. If you need to brag a little now, no one will mind.

Jupiter Successful expansion of the mind, education goes well, successful communication, a fortunate idea, overcoming all obstacles to education or travel. Successfully defending your thesis.

Saturn Overcoming all stress or worry, your goals are protected, mental achievement, the writing gets done, the project is complete, your hard work pays off handsomely.

Uranus Sudden successful ideas, successful writing, publishing, marketing, meeting last minute deadlines with flair.

Neptune Receiving psychic messages, automatic writing, channeled wisdom, hidden or spiritual information is uncovered and brings insights that protect you, angelic guidance overcomes all challenges now.

Pluto Deep, intense thinking, a probing mind helps you to overcome all problems, challenges lead to insight, transforming the self by harnessing the power of the mind.

SUMMARY: The theme of the reading is success with all types of communication. Writing, speaking, teaching and all mental pursuits go well and you have the ability to deliver powerful messages. Your ideas flow easily, you are articulate, and interesting conversations ensue. The mind is well balanced now, and your ideas are well protected.

BIRTH CARD: If the 8 ♣ is your Birth Card, yours is the power of ideas. Developing a powerful mind, along with the proper use of knowledge, will be a major part of your life. Dealing with powerful ideas, but in a balanced way, grants you a great deal of protection in life. Because you can overcome all oppositions to your ideas, and push them past any objections to your plans, you must first be sure that your ideas are worthy. Your strong will combined with a rational and sensible approach, will bring happiness and success both personally and professionally.

✦ *Eight of Diamonds* ✦

Mercury Overcoming obstacles to your money-making ideas, "get rich quick" schemes might actually work now, a valuable idea, a quick profit, walking your talk when it comes to what you value. The financial news is all good.

Venus Money comes in and you can spend it if you want to. Protection for the home, for resources and for all you value. Work parties succeed, clients chose you. Sitting pretty. Protection for family legacies.

Mars Overcoming all challenges or challengers, winning the top prize. Taking home the gold. You crow like a rooster and the crowd cheers. Your passion and drive pay off, quick money. Making the payoff look easy.

Jupiter Total protection for your finances, an opportunity presents itself to take a valuable trip, money available for expansion, travel or education.

Saturn Your salary/bank account/investments are protected, overcoming all obstacles to achievement and promotion, work goes well and past efforts are rewarded. Working steadily and patiently towards your goals. What you purchase now accrues in value over time.

Uranus New clients, eclectic people favor you now, money made thru astrology, metaphysics or thru an unusual job, a new age business, funds become suddenly available in the strangest ways.

Neptune Your financial intuition is spot on, heed it. Have faith that all is secure. Belief in your own talents and abilities brings financial success. You are priceless. Believe it.

Pluto A deep inner value system transforms you and keeps you grounded. Something substantial to build upon, a solid foundation. Big business, a large amount of money, financial power, many clients.

SUMMARY: The theme of the reading is protection in all of your financial interactions and you have the ability to create or broker powerful deals. You are blessed now with an inner knowing or understanding that all is safe and secure. Your core values are built on a solid foundation. Overall, this is a time to enjoy prosperity and abundance.

BIRTH CARD: If the 8 ♦ is your Birth Card, then yours is the power of resources (and resourcefulness). At some point you will feel the need to work out issues around the balance of power, and this will be a major part of your life. Recognizing that true power doesn't come from money but from within creates true security. Creating a solid sense of your own self worth will provide you with the core inner strength required for your mission, but you must deal with financial issues honestly and in a timely manner. Dealing with the concept of prosperity or issues of financial power in a balanced way allows you to enjoy a protected life. Your strong will combined with a value-added approach, will bring happiness and success both personally and professionally.

♠ *Eight of Spades* ♠

Mercury Mind over Matter. Good news. Communications succeed and are well received now, discussions are illuminating. Computer work goes well, protection for your ideas, your data is secure. Health is protected.

Venus Your relationships are protected (or they protect you), relationships with women go especially well, your home and family are safe and secure.

Mars Confidently taking on the competition...and winning, a new challenge is invigorating, relationships with men go well, confidence and courage are yours now. Your health is stable and strong. Dodging the bullet.

Jupiter Health and work opportunities expand, health improvements, your trip is safe, studies go well, overcoming all problems. All roads take you where you want to go now.

Saturn Your job is protected now, your health and work life improve through your own hard work. Your efforts succeed. Overcoming challenges at work, achievement is secured.

Uranus Someone unexpectedly protects you, suddenly overcoming a challenge (or challenger), a surprise victory, coming from behind, turning a corner, sudden recovery.

Neptune Your hunches are correct, follow them and they will protect and guide you now, inner strength, spiritual direction. The rebirth of a vision for your career or ideas for the renewal of your health.

Pluto Strong willpower available to overcome any health or work issues. Challenged to use the strength of your will to best effect by creating a strong career path and excellent health in your life.

SUMMARY: The theme of the reading is protection for your health and you have the ability to create a more powerful physical vessel. Any outstanding or chronic health issues can be successfully dealt with or overcome now and the proper treatment can finally be found. Your career is also on solid ground and you are financially protected. Overall, this is a time to enjoy success, security and good health.

BIRTH CARD: If the 8 ♠ is your Birth Card, then yours is the power of purpose. At some point there will awaken in you a strong sense of destiny or purpose and developing this will be a major part of your life. Creating vibrant physical health will provide the stamina you require for your mission and so you must deal with health issues in a timely manner. This allows you to enjoy a protected life. Your strong will combined with a sense of divine spiritual purpose, will bring happiness and success both personally and professionally.

Nines

The Nines represent endings. Something is finished, done, over, completed. You are either breaking something off or graduating to the next level of achievement or experience. The cycle has come full circle and is now closed.

All Nines contain some measure of trial and tribulation and require personal sacrifice to process. There is also the theme of purging or "getting rid of" with the Nines. And, for the most part, there is no "in-between" with them. You either take the high road or the low road: you fly with the eagles or fall to the depths. Keep in mind that both roads have their own lessons to teach. Of all the cards to use in prediction, I sometimes think that the Nines are the hardest of all.

For instance, the 9 ♠ is the only card I use for physical disability or death–although it does not always mean death–you have to read the cards around it to interpret it correctly! Always interpret the Nines with care. Just know, that the Nines are not always scary. For instance, Nines may appear in your reading to represent a happy completion of a long term project or a successful graduation from school. As with all cards, your attitude when interpreting them, is just as important as the event being interpreted.

♥ Nine of Hearts ♥

Mercury Finishing the course, the end of the talks, heartfelt disappointment, separation or divorce papers. Processing your disappointment.

Venus The divorce card or the card of separation from loved ones. Saying goodbye, the loss of a loved one. Parting is such sweet sorrow, leaving home, seeing the last of her (or him). Emotional sacrifice, release, letting go. Parenting ends–your job is done, loving unconditionally.

Mars An emotional parting, ending the affair, a speedy ending, culling the herd, seeing the last of him (or her), an angry ending, good riddance. Ending family relationship patterns.

Jupiter A successful conclusion, an emotionally satisfying ending, loving from a distance, graduation, projects finished successfully, happily releasing what (or who) needs to go.

Saturn Difficult loss, depression. Working hard at networking, firing someone/letting someone go. New people come with responsibilities—stick with those you already know. Friends at work are hard to find, mixing business and pleasure must be done carefully. Sometimes the hardest part about being a father is knowing when to stop giving advice. They'll ask if they need it.

Uranus A quick exit, a sudden or unexpected parting of the ways, a sudden disappointment or loss, working for a heartfelt cause, sacrificing for a higher purpose, an unexpected gift (someone else makes a sacrifice for you).

Neptune Foreseeing the ending, finishing with unconditional love and acceptance. Parting by taking the high road, releasing your love, a spiritual end, disillusionment, the dream ends. Releasing toxic people. It doesn't necessarily hurt less just because you know it's coming, but it does give you time to prepare.

Pluto A cycle of love is completed, deep or intense personal release. Saying goodbye after release can transform you, as well as the person released, releasing family to their highest good. Letting go is inevitable now, but the sooner you do it, the less it will hurt.

SUMMARY: The theme of the reading is saying goodbye. This is a time of emotional release, with all its many challenges. Release now will lead to healing and, eventually, to the ability to love again. You may be called upon to sacrifice your needs for the good of the community, but this gives you the opportunity to serve humanity on a higher level. This is the time to consciously purge people from your life that no longer belong there or who no longer serve your highest good.

BIRTH CARD: If the 9 ♥ is your Birth Card, an important part of your life path will involve important personal endings or the transformation of yourself through love. Your life will, quite literally, be about those you love and sometimes about those you love and lose. And it is vital that you act responsibly in all relationships. Nevertheless, much can be accomplished as a result. You are in the process of tying up loose ends in your relations with others, some of which may have been left undone from previous lifetimes. Purging attachment to those who are no longer appropriate is an important process. Disappointment is sometimes associated with the 9 ♥, and yours is a life of personal sacrifice, but that is only because you have such high ideals. You see the potential for how people should treat one another, and if you find the right group to work with, you may help bring that vision to life. Whatever path you choose, your goal will be to completely dedicate yourself in service to universal love, and you will sometimes lose yourself in the process. You are working not for your own good, but for the good of all. The primary need here is to help others before you help yourself, so in immersing yourself, you are found.

♣ *Nine of Clubs* ♣

Mercury Canceling the meeting, making sacrifices for your ideas, breaking the contract, saying "goodbye" (literally), the end of the conversation, "irreconcilable differences," it's all been said before, having the last word, finishing your thought, the final word, the last chapter of the book, "the last thing I said to him/her was..."

Venus The chatter has finally stopped, parting in silence. Can be either a quiet home or a celebration (depending on you). The end of the friendship, a parting of the ways, releasing the past (or the people in it). Finishing up your writing projects. A note of farewell.

Mars An end to passion, a quick or angry parting, words aren't helpful (or aren't enough), unplugging the phone, the talks end. Taking a much-needed break, the mind needs rest, energy may be in short supply now. The project is either wrapped up quickly or the idea dies, last minute cancellations. A hasty departure.

Jupiter Graduation! Your studies have concluded, final exams, defending your thesis, an advanced degree, the results are in. Completing a writing project, the book is done. A fortunate ending, the trip is over, the road stops here.

Saturn A depressed mind doesn't work well, challenging health problem or work situation, outdated processes don't help things, unemployment. Concluding past responsibilities works better now than taking on new ones. Finish up then take a break.

Uranus Blurting something out that ends things between you, spontaneously telling it like it is. Donating your time or ideas to others.

Neptune A spiritual cycle completes itself in your life, a complete vision. The pilgrimage ends. You wake up from the dream. Where to next? Rest up and think about it.

Pluto Challenged to release old or limiting thought patterns, certain ideas have outgrown their usefulness, new ideas will change your life—after you let go of the old ones.

SUMMARY: The theme of the reading is mental release and the challenges associated with it. This is the time to let go of certain negative or incorrect thought patterns that have held you back. Letting go of the past can free you up to start over. Old philosophies or outmoded ways of thinking will end now, so that new ideas can begin. Changing your mind now can literally change your life.

BIRTH CARD: If the 9 ♣ is your Birth Card, an important part of your life path will involve the end of a way of thinking or believing. Your life will be about finishing things in one way or another and much can be accomplished as a result. And it is vital that you complete your education. Whether completing projects or your ideas, you are in the process of finishing your thoughts, some of which may have been left undone from previous lifetimes. Purging irrelevant or incorrect ideas or belief systems is an important process for you. Disappointment is sometimes associated with the 9 ♣, and yours is a life of mental sacrifice, but that is only because you have such high ideals. You see the potential for how thoughts should manifest, and if you find the right venue you may help bring that vision to life. Whatever path you choose, your goal will be to completely dedicate yourself in service to universal knowledge, and you will sometimes lose yourself in the process. You are working not for your own good, but for the good of all. The primary need here is to help others before you help yourself, so in immersing yourself, you are found.

Mercury A short trip to the bank (or "breaking the bank"), wills, sorting thru your valuables (or what's of value to you), a final evaluation. Completely letting go of old attitudes about money. The job doesn't come thru, but perhaps it wasn't the job for you. Hearing news of loss.

Venus A large sum of money goes out, purchasing gifts for family or friends, spending on the home, needing a large sum. The request for a raise is declined. Wait it out (or try another job). Prosperity will cycle around again.

Mars A large sum quickly spent, a major purchase, easy come, easy go, only spend what you can afford now. The complete cycle of money as energy.

Jupiter Inheritance, profit from loss, someone else's loss might be your gain now, a large tax return, spending a large amount, an important purchase or payment, a large sum (or gift) appears when you need it, an expensive trip or education.

Saturn A sacrifice of time or resources. Repaying large debts, end of the year taxes, real estate finances. Either selling (leaving) a home or purchasing a home (leaving the old one behind). Assistance ends, but then again, so may poverty.

Uranus An unexpectedly large bill, loosing something of value, the job suddenly ends. Money going out, bills being dealt with late or at the last minute, charitable donations, giving to a cause.

Neptune "If wishes were horses, beggars would ride", dreaming of a fortune, charitable contributions. A spiritual view of money flowing outward towards its highest application. Letting go of the material in favor of the spiritual.

Pluto Challenged or empowered to give freely without expectation of return. Pay what you owe and give the rest away, releasing what you no longer need will free you in the end.

SUMMARY: The theme of the reading is the release of your resources and the trials and challenges associated with it. Money may actually need to flow out now, and trying to stop it may just be counterproductive. Either way, you are likely to be making financial sacrifices for others who are less fortunate or less able. In certain cases this card can also indicate a loss of income (check the cards surrounding it). Use any cost-cutting measures available to you now: cut the fat from the budget, do without (or make do). And when you do give, give freely, without strings attached. La Fortuna goes up, La Fortuna goes down. It's a cycle. In the end, it's all about knowing what is truly important. Those who know what has real value to them will be just fine.

BIRTH CARD: If the 9 ♦ is your Birth Card, an important part of your life path will involve important financial endings or the completion of some major goals related to values (or what one perceives to be valuable). Your life will be about giving things away and providing for the security of others, and in this respect, philanthropy will take you much farther than feathering your own nest. And it is vital that you pay all your debts. If you choose to hide or hoard resources, it makes no difference. The money will flow out regardless, and you'll be right back to where you began. You are in the process of strengthening your own value system and completing a cycle of evaluating self worth, which may have been only partially formed in previous lifetimes. Seeing the things that money can't buy (love, security, loyalty) is just as important as seeing the good it can do. Disappointment is sometimes associated with the 9♦, and yours is a life of financial sacrifice, but that is only because you have such high ideals. You see the potential for what should have value, and if you find the right career, you may help bring that vision to life. Whatever path you choose, your goal will be to completely dedicate yourself to a higher system of universal values, and you will sometimes lose yourself in the process. You are working not for your own good, but for the good of all. The primary need here is to help others before you help yourself, so in immersing yourself, you are found.

Mercury A troubled mind, stroke, dementia, a long memory coming to an end, writing a will or health proxy, discussing the end of things, misplaced letters, lost data, stolen information, identity theft, completing your education (the training wheels are removed).

Venus The aging process for women, the loss of a friend or family member, reproductive health, female menopause, the end of her, a loving end or the end of love.

Mars The aging process for men, the loss of a partner, sexual health, male menopause, the end of him, an angry ending, a passionate finish, an energetic finale. The job or situation ends quickly. Making fast work of it.

Jupiter A fortunate or auspicious ending, the results of physical or health changes, contemplating the path not taken, the road not traveled...but then you begin again. Unpacking and putting down roots instead.

Saturn The aging process (of both people and things), everything has a life cycle. Finishing up old business, the project concludes, finishing the job, ending a career, retirement, seeing something thru to the very end, concluding past responsibilities. Serious illness, a difficult loss, death of an older person, grief, funerals, a final farewell, over and done, good and gone, over and out.

Uranus A sudden exit or death, unexpectedly quitting your job (or getting fired), donating your talents, working for a non-profit or for a cause (as in "to end" something...hunger, poverty, abuse, etc.).

Neptune A confusing end to things (or "no end in sight"), drug or alcohol overdose, water in the lungs, "a watery grave," your boat has sunk. A spiritual ending, leaving the church, the initiate becomes the guru, final vows.

Pluto The death card (or dealing with your fear of death or the unknown). Purging health habits, physical transformation and release, the aging process, life, death, rebirth—the cycle of life, processing loss or grief, transformed by endings, something has completed, a permanent change.

SUMMARY: The theme of the reading is physical release–something dies, something is reborn and the cycle of life continues. This is a time for recognizing the aging process and for processing physical decline (and/or what you can and can't do about it or control). It is a good time to focus on physical "purging" with respect to both your body and your stuff. As you release unnecessary items, detrimental habit patterns may also be released. The purpose is to gain greater understanding of the connection between what you do every day and how it either contributes to your health or to your demise, and this may include your health routines, levels of stress, negative vs positive thought patterns, etc. This card signals the end of a matter of importance. Whether the ending is experienced as positive or negative depends entirely upon your outlook.

BIRTH CARD: If the 9 ♠ is your Birth Card, an important part of your life path will involve important endings or graduations, which may be intense or even dramatic at times. Your life will be about finishing things in one way or another and much can be accomplished as a result. Whether completing projects or your education, you are in the process of tying up loose ends, some of which may have been left undone from previous lifetimes. And it is also vital that you respect your body and take responsibility for your health. Purging negative or useless habit patterns, especially with regard to health, is an important process. Disappointment is sometimes associated with the 9 ♠, and yours is a life of sacrifice of your labor, but that is only because you have such high ideals. You see the potential for how things should be, and if you find the right purpose, you may help bring that vision to life. Whatever path you choose, your goal will be to completely dedicate yourself in service to a universal cause, and you will sometimes lose yourself in the process. You are working not for your own good, but for the good of all. The primary need here is to help others before you help yourself, so in immersing yourself, you are found.

Tens

♥ ♣ ♦ ♠ ♥ ♣ ♦ ♠

After the completion of the cycle of 9 come the TENS. The TENS bring us full circle (1+0=1 again), except on a higher level, because this time around it comes with all the experience gleaned from numbers 1 thru 9.

The Tens represent "many" (as opposed to "a few") or a large amount of something. And all Tens will "live life large" to some extent. They generally have an entourage of people, a plethora of ideas, multiple income streams, and/or opportunities galore surrounding them at all times. In other words, they tend to juggle a lot of balls in the air at once!

Success certainly can be sweet for the Tens. The caution for them is in overdoing it, because they tend to want to expand too rapidly. In so doing, there is the danger of collapse, but also they may just be moving so quickly that they take all of their many successes for granted.

♥ *Ten of Hearts* ♥

Mercury Letters of recommendation, good news, heartfelt communication, talking about love, happy chatter, surrounded by good wishes, lots of people coming and going bringing good cheer. Ban gossip.

Venus Social cliques, charm and charisma, you are blessed to be loved by many, friends and family wish you well, if throwing a party, expect a crowd—everyone will bring a "plus one."

Mars Persuasive salesmanship, lots of energy to fulfill your most heartfelt desires, you got "game," passions rule the day and win the crowd over, celebrations and parties.

Jupiter Social climbing, hobnobbing, rubbing elbows with the elite, surrounded by successful or highly placed people, socializing leads to success, you may need crowd control.

Saturn Successful people give you the thumbs-up and help you get ahead, your reputation precedes you and can open doors, success at work with coworkers, employees, and higher ups, the leader of men, the diplomat, the successful "people person."

Uranus An unexpected or last minute invitation to the palace, dress for success! A flash mob. A surprise party—and you're the guest of honor, a surprising display of affection, a surprise gift, a group gift.

Neptune Make a wish, then dress like Cinderella 'cuz you're going to the ball! A successful launch, a lovely cruise with lots of company, a successful metaphysical or spiritual gathering. Putting your whole heart and soul into your projects makes them an even bigger success.

Pluto Challenged to keep your social calendar from blowing up, too much of a good thing is fabulous (and intense). Everyone loves you, popularity. A reminder: Family is there for you when no one else will be; but we can all still find it challenging to appreciate them properly every now and again. Once you've reached the top, don't forget the ones who helped you get there. Realizing you are wanted can be a transformational experience.

SUMMARY: The theme of the reading is social success. This is a time for feeling valued and appreciated, as love comes to you many times over now. It is likely you will find yourself surrounded by friends and family, as you enjoy gifts, get-togethers and displays of affection. Many people will freely offer you their trust now. Remember to keep confidences private in order to retain your successful reputation.

BIRTH CARD: If the 10 ♥ is your Birth Card, successful relationships will be an important part of your life path. This Ten values love and kindness for all and recognizes that real love is unconditional. And if your love is true, you will enjoy harmonious interactions with friends and family. Sometimes you may be tempted to try to "save" everyone you love, and you can collect quite an entourage! The ability to juggle many relationship balls at one time comes naturally to you, however with access to such a high level of success, you may overdo it. One of your life lessons may be to learn to prioritize your relationships, so that those people who are truly important to you may receive your best efforts. For in the end you come to know, that love is all, the rest is show.

Mercury Successful communication and self-promotion, writing, teaching or speaking goes well, talking to a crowd, your book hits the bestseller's list, avoid the water cooler talk (don't gossip).

Venus A successful outing or social gathering, attending important events, hosting a successful party, lots of people to talk to, your home is the center of the conversation.

Mars Success with physical and mental pursuits, aggressively pitching your ideas to the boss, persuasive conversation, ambitious notions.

Jupiter Lots of students, successful lectures, many trips planned, a full itinerary, pack your bags! Or do you prefer to be an armchair traveler?

Saturn Multiple business proposals at once, career success, handling responsibilities well, the expert in his/her field. An excellent professional reputation.

Uranus Numerous exciting and successful ideas, marketing and promotions go well, last minute meetings or decisions go your way. The tide turns in your favor. A spontaneous photo op.

Neptune Making your hopes and dreams come true, successful spiritual talks or writing, a fair wind fills your sails. Combining smarts with imagination wins every time.

Pluto Challenged to communicate well. Becoming the best teacher, speaker or writer you can be, successful communications transform you. Powerful ideas, convincing speeches, your words reach a large audience. The crowd cheers. Friends with strong opinions.

SUMMARY: The theme of the reading is successful communication. This is the time for interesting conversations, where many ideas can be exchanged and shared. You have the gift of gab now, and you can put it to good use while networking or at social get-togethers. It is likely that you will be surrounded by like-minded people who enjoy your wit and wisdom. Your company is sought after. It is possible that others may "over-share" now. As for yourself, say just enough.

BIRTH CARD: If the 10 ♣ is your Birth Card, success in communication will be an important part of your life path. You will naturally gravitate to careers involving speaking, writing, teaching and networking. It's also possible that your career may involve delivering an important message of your own. Whether socializing or in business meetings, you must beware of over talking; listening should be at least half of every conversation you take part in. You will also have a tendency to over schedule yourself. The ability to juggle many mental balls at one time comes naturally to you, however, with access to such a high level of success, you may overdo it. One of your life lessons may be to learn to prioritize your time, so that the ideas that are truly important to you may receive your best efforts. For in the end you come to know, that reason is all, the rest is show.

◆ *Ten of Diamonds* ◆

Mercury Good financial news, words are prosperous now. Talking to others about how to be financially successful, jobs that pay well. Don't brag (openly) about your pay raise around the office.

Venus Spending a large amount on your home and family, money to spend on luxury items, successful home business, money-making ideas.

Mars Energetically pursuing what you want, your popularity is enhanced, self-employment, salesmanship.

Jupiter A large amount of money, financial success, a raise, winnings, hitting the Jackpot! A generous gift (given or received). Count your blessings—they are many.

Saturn Hard work pays off with career advancement, financial responsibilities are all fulfilled, bills are marked "paid in full," entering a higher tax bracket, paying or collecting debts, the CFO.

Uranus A big financial surprise, an unexpected bonus check, an on line auction with many bidders. The early bird gets the worm.

Neptune Lots of psychic or metaphysical clients, a seaworthy vessel, dreaming of financial success. Putting your money (and your time and effort) where your dreams are makes them come true.

Pluto Financial success transforms your life and opens up lots of possibilities for the future, doors open before you. Does your new success challenge you to be a better person? Friends with influence.

SUMMARY: The theme of the reading is financial success and the ability to live prosperously. You may be able to help a multitude of people by sharing your own personal values. It is likely that you will either be exposed to, or surrounded by, a culture of wealth. Discretion will be required with all financial data you have access to (yours as well as others).

BIRTH CARD: If the 10 ♦ is your Birth Card, successful finances will be an important part of your life path. Beware of over spending or overextending yourself financially. The ability to juggle many financial balls at one time comes naturally to you, however, with access to such a high level of success, you may overdo it. One of your life lessons may be to learn to prioritize your financial goals, so that what is truly important to you may receive your best efforts. For in the end you come to know, that your values are all, the rest is show.

♠ *Ten of Spades* ♠

Mercury Successful communication with coworkers (or a lot of gossip!), lots of conversation with employees and those in charge, healthy routines, keep proprietary data to yourself at work.

Venus Happiness with family and friends, success follows the smart money, lots of social interaction, people power, strong physical health.

Mars Physical stamina, tons of energy, virility, the boy's club, physical strength, pedal to the metal. Success follows your passion and drive—get out there and get busy!

Jupiter Successful expansion of your business, lots of successful work coming in, more clients, successful classes. Mentoring others, a good example (as opposed to "a cautionary tale"). Good news about a health matter.

Saturn "Large and In Charge." Your past hard work and effort pay off big time now, you're at the top of your game and can handle whatever comes. Excellent PR. Your reputation precedes you. The boss, the authority, CEO.

Uranus Unexpected or sudden success with a work or health matter, sudden opportunities, an unusual amount of success may be yours, the early bird gets the worm.

Neptune Anchors away. Blue skies and clear sailing! The Yachtsman. Successful metaphysical work, charitable projects succeed. Excellent health means more energy for success.

Pluto The challenge is to handle this level of success with grace and style—you can do it! Good health and work habits can have a transformational effect on your lifestyle. Your reputation may reach far and wide now. Friends in high places.

SUMMARY: The theme of the reading is the enjoyment of overall success in life. This is a time of good health, successful work, and enjoyable projects. You can also count on being able to combine business and pleasure well now. You are on the winning team! And you are likely to be surrounded by coworkers or employees who think the world of you. You can repay the compliment by keep their confidences.

BIRTH CARD: If the 10 ♠ is your Birth Card, work and service will be an important part of your life path. Beware of overwork or taking on more projects than you can effectively manage or finish on time. All Tens do have the ability to keep many balls in the air at one time, however, with access to such a high level of success, you may overdo it. One of your life lessons may be to learn to prioritize your energy, so that those projects that are truly important to you may receive your best efforts. For in the end you come to know, that purpose is all, the rest is show.

The Royal Court Cards

The Jacks, Queens, and Kings represent the Royal Court and as such they may be held to a somewhat higher standard. This is especially true if one of them is your Birth Card. The Jacks, or Knaves, are generally seen as soldiers or servants and are not part of the royal family by blood. But though they may be of lower rank, they serve their King and Queen with distinction and are therefore considered an indispensable part of the Royal Court.

All Royals will have their own personal courts and subjects who surround them. In that respect they are somewhat fortunate, because they can look to those that surround them as a kind of barometer or benchmark for their own success. In other words, their success or failure as rulers will be mirrored in those they rule. The one problem with the court cards is that they have few real peers, not to mention that getting the crown is not the same thing as keeping the crown! "Uneasy the head that wears the crown," or "it's lonely at the top," are but two sayings which may help to summarize some of the problems of royalty.

Still and all, "It's Good to be the King (or Queen)!" is also a saying, and as the Royals are the ones who make the rules, they will have their say. The King and Queen do seem to enjoy a certain amount of privilege in one or more areas, and an air of entitlement seems to accompany them. But with that entitlement comes great responsibility.

Kings and Queens are kept busy upholding the responsibilities of running the Kingdom and making sure that their subjects are well provided for. Should their subjects become restless or unhappy, woe betide them. Because all royal cards, to some extent, depend upon their subjects, just as their subjects depend upon them. In that respect, one can say there is a symbiotic link between them.

It is also important to mention–that while Kings represent masculine or active traits and Queens represent feminine or passive traits–men can still be "Queens" and woman can still be "Kings." These are not gender-specific cards. Students have often asked me what the difference is between them.

The King and Queen are *equal* in power, but are not the *same*. This is an important distinction, because they each have their own individual contributions to make to "the Kingdom" (ie: society), but they will make those contributions in different ways. The King represents the Divine Masculine principle. His contribution is active in nature:

leading, protecting, defending. The Queen represents the Divine Feminine principle, and her contribution is passive in nature: nurturing, teaching, guiding. They both represent maturity, they both rule, they both carry authority, but they apply their skills differently.

It's also important to note that they need one another. A King without his Queen is unbalanced and incomplete, and vice versa. An out of balance King or Queen is likely to be cranky, overly critical, egotistical and arrogant.

The Divine Couple, the God and the Goddess, the Sun and the Moon–however you prefer to think of them as archetypes–the King and Queen are meant to work in unison, and they are strongest when they do.

The happiest Court Cards are those who have learned to rule benevolently. They fill their days nurturing, protecting and growing their kingdoms. The least happy Court Cards are the ones who have failed or ignored their subjects. They enjoy all the privilege while ignoring all the duties. These eventually become the exiled Kings and Queens, without a kingdom at all.

Jacks

The Jacks (or Elevens) represent youth and its exuberance for life. Jacks can be witty, clever and very creative. The term "Jack of all trades" fits them, as they are versatile, adaptable, and even somewhat like chameleons. They make excellent salesman, but they must take care lest their youth, inexperience or naiveté cause them to be less than honest with themselves or others.

Because they are so charming, all Jacks can get away with more than they should. Also, they can be tricksters, and one must safeguard one's identity around the more slippery Jack types. In the workplace, as in life, Jacks are "hands-on" and many of them will be self-employed (even while working for others!). They rely primarily on their own unique talents and abilities, and are adept multi-taskers who will always have many side projects. Jacks are also known as soldiers, and they serve and protect their King and Queen with honor and skill.

Jacks can be male or female and have a somewhat androgynous quality, but they generally tend to represent youth–children, young adults, siblings or cousins. The true Jack is like Peter Pan, eternally youthful and creative regardless of age, or, as Wendy says to Peter at the end of the book: "Oh! The Cleverness of Youth!"

But the highest possible expression for a Jack is one of personal sacrifice, the type of sacrifice one makes as an idealistic youth who believes wholeheartedly in a cause. If your reading contains multiple Jacks you will likely spend some time with children or young adults; or you will have a time of developing your own creativity in a youthful manner.

♥ *Jack of Hearts* ♥

Mercury Listening to others, sacrificing for siblings or cousins, educating yourself about a specific cause, emotion-fueled beliefs, one-sided or emotion-fueled beliefs, mercurial ideas, writing beautiful thoughts.

Venus Sacrifices made for love or family, or allowances made because of their youth and inexperience. Young love, immature love, besotted, in love with love, manipulating the emotions of others, being fleet of heart, lighthearted, young at heart, spending time with young people, happy with your creative efforts, making beautiful things! The Princess Bride.

Mars High Road: sacrificing personal desires. Low Road: pushing your own agenda at everyone else's expense. The energy and drive of youth, first sexual experience, first love, feeling like a kid again, enjoying youthful company. Dealing with children or young adults.

Jupiter Sacrifices made for educational pursuits, the education of the young, making a trip for someone else, travel that makes the heart lighter. Visiting beautiful places, a creative vacation.

Saturn Charity work, relationships are hard work now—are they worth it? Having to grow up. The process of entering adulthood. Learning to love what you do, being mentored by a friend or family member. Learning the ropes by climbing them.

Uranus Either giving up personal freedom for a higher purpose, or demanding it for yourself, Rebel Without a Cause? A sudden party invite. Network! Spontaneous beauty.

Neptune Spiritual sacrifices, taking the high road, intuitive children, possible deception in love, idealized love, the spiritual initiate. Spiritual beauty.

Pluto Following your inner child, or a higher calling in all your important relationships with others, one way or another—love and beauty can be transformational now. Being genuine with others.

SUMMARY: The theme of the reading is young love with all its inherent sweetness and bittersweet heartache. It shows the timeless appeal of the boy or girl next door: forever youthful, forever beautiful. This may also indicate the necessity, at times, of making sacrifices (or allowances) for the young, and there may be dealings with children, teens or young adults. Or, a young person may discover an important cause close to their heart. And lastly, it is a reminder that our creativity keeps us all young at heart, no matter your age!

BIRTH CARD: If the Jack ♥ is your Birth Card, you will sacrifice everything for true love. The trick is finding it. And you will enjoy expressing your creativity through youthful relationships. But you may find it challenging to give your heart away. Expanding your ever-widening circle of friends and acquaintances and developing your relationships can literally keep you feeling young and vital regardless of your true age. But you'll live only for yourself until you find someone you truly love.

♣ *Jack of Clubs* ♣

Mercury A ready wit and silver tongue, important personal beliefs, mental creativity, originality, getting on a soapbox, the young writer or speaker, writing children's stories, identity theft, learning the difference between networking and gossip.

Venus Social charm, partying, social life, youthful get-togethers, working or playing creatively in a home studio, staying too long at the fair.

Mars Charisma, sexual attraction, mental energy on overdrive—careful that boredom doesn't lead you down the wrong path—channel your energies into creative adventures! The mind is very active now, ideas flow quickly. Inspiring the young (or young at heart).

Jupiter Fortunate creative ideas, successful writing projects, sales ability, too much of a good thing, youthful enthusiasm. Students suddenly appear.

Saturn Working hard at creative projects, coming up with original ideas takes effort now but originality has its own rewards, communicating responsibly with those who are younger or less experienced, sage advice for the young. Tricking others into doing your work has its consequences.

Uranus Creative genius, sudden brilliant ideas, extreme creativity, playing hooky. An unexpected day off...make the most of it!

Neptune Great imagination, successful songwriters and musicians, inspirational or devotional music or poetry, successful creative projects, fooling no one so much as yourself.

Pluto Developing your own unique creative ideas will transform you, the wisdom of just being yourself soon becomes clear to you.

SUMMARY: The theme of the reading is the mental vibrancy and flexibility (or even changeability) of youth. It may seem at times as though the world is chock full of brilliant creative ideas and you are like Columbus discovering and mapping out the new world! It's exciting but also as yet undiscovered. The act of uncovering the mystery is what interests you. Knowing which ideas are timely now will lead you to greater success. You may decide to take a more youthful and original approach to life. Or you may be involved in writing children's stories or corresponding with young people.

BIRTH CARD: If the Jack ♣ is your Birth Card, you will sacrifice everything for the right idea. The trick is believing in it. And you will enjoy expressing your creativity through a youthful mind. But you may find it challenging to live by any belief system. Expanding your knowledge base and developing your mind can literally keep you feeling young and vital regardless of your true age. You are likely to think only of yourself until you find someone more interesting.

◆ *Jack of Diamonds* ◆

Mercury The thief or gambler's card. Can also be a slick con-man. Playing fast and loose with the funds. Risking it all, betting the house on it. Creative writing or marketing, original ideas pay off, young people, getting or giving good financial advice, discussions about self-worth or what you value. A fast talker, taking more than you're due.

Venus Your charisma sells it now, earning power, sales ability, marketing, financial creativity. The profit lies with those you know (and those who know you), your reputation is important here—guard it.

Mars Marketing yourself, making things, creative advertising campaigns, financially creative energy, believing in your talents and abilities, aggressive salesmanship, being pushy in order to seal the deal (channeling your inner used-car salesman?). But remember, it's your passion that sells it.

Jupiter Money to travel, a fun, youthful vacation or get-away, students, money for education, studying abroad, the traveling salesman, a young person goes far (or travels far). Money made thru creative efforts.

Saturn Working hard to create something of value, creative ideas may be costly now or take a long time to develop. It's creative, but is it practical? Earning money the old fashioned way—working for it, inventive and persistent salesmanship. Bringing your ideas and plans to the next level; your creative ideas mature, financial mentor-ship, lessons about the value of money. A first real job.

Uranus Unexpected success or sudden theft. Used car sales? Keep your wits about you. Creative marketing, sudden financial opportunities.

Neptune Stick to your own spiritual value system now—it will take you far, integrity wins out.

Pluto Learning to value yourself and your own talents and abilities will transform you and create financial success. Realizing that you are more than enough.

SUMMARY: The theme of the reading is one of self-discovery–the picture of youth, as it grows into young adulthood. You may be discovering your true values for the first time, along with the realization that what we desire and what we value are not always the same thing. You may be earning your first paycheck at this time, or just contemplating your potential worth.

BIRTH CARD: If the Jack ♦ is your Birth Card, you will sacrifice everything for security. The trick is what it will cost you. And you will enjoy expressing your creativity through youthful values. But you may find it challenging to live up to the right values. Discovering and developing your own talents and abilities can literally keep you feeling young and vital regardless of your true age. You are likely to rely solely on your own resources until you find someone richer (or more talented).

♠ *Jack of Spades* ♠

Mercury A potential liar's card. Can also be the actor or story teller's card. Extreme creativity at work, mental gymnastics, marketing and sales, ideas put to the test, stretching the truth. The true Jack of all Trades.

Venus Creative ideas for combining business and pleasure (or, your business is pleasure). Working with family, expressing one's creativity in the home, creative projects with family and friends. Feeling like a kid again.

Mars Competition may be stiff, but you're more clever than that. Creative energy to be the best, winning, youthful exuberance, the need for speed.

Jupiter A trip may inspire creativity or project ideas, hands-on learning, learning by doing, on-the-job training, vocational school. Creative employment.

Saturn Working at a creative profession, beating the competition through hard work and creative ideas, being mentored by someone older and wiser. Pay attention and you'll learn something new.

Uranus Taking a risk. An unexpected creative job offer or the sudden loss of a job (Jacks can go either way—ask yourself if it's the RIGHT job for YOU), a medical test is revealing, sudden insight.

Neptune Spiritual sacrifices, taking the high road, the spiritual initiate, secret knowledge, channeling divine inspiration, following a guru. Intuition around a work or health-related matter. Intuitive children, meditations for the young. Idealized love, the complete conviction of youthful belief–like Peter Pan bringing Tinker Bell back from the dead: *I do believe in fairies! I do! I do!*

Pluto Working thru your creative blocks leads to intense creative breakthroughs, and ultimately, success. Your work is exciting now, even with all the hurdles you are jumping! The health and work habits you develop now will either help or hinder you later, so do it right.

SUMMARY: The theme of the reading is creativity in action and you will strive for originality in all your work. You are in the process of discovering what your path is meant to be. Your health will also benefit from a creative and youthful approach now. You may look and feel younger than you are!

BIRTH CARD: If the Jack ♠ is your Birth Card, you will sacrifice everything for the right purpose. The trick is having faith. And you will enjoy expressing your creativity with youthful work. But until you can trust in the process you will find it difficult to really commit to the end. The right work can literally keep you feeling young and vital regardless of your true age, and you'll likely work only for yourself until you find someone more worthy.

Queens

The Queens (or Twelves) represent maturity and femininity. They are the model of motherhood and unconditional love, and embody the qualities of patience and kindness. They nurture others in body and soul and make excellent teachers or spiritual guides. On an esoteric level, they represent the Goddess and the Divine Feminine.

Queens are usually women, however they can also just represent those qualities generally associated with women, as either gender may encompass both male and female traits. In general though, the Queens usually represent mothers or mature women and/or women in authority. However, one exception to this general rule is if any of the Queen cards happens to be your personal Birth Card (and you can look up your Birth Card in the section entitled *Your Birth Card*).

Let's say, for example, that you were born on January 2nd of any year. That would make your birthcard the Queen of Spades. Obviously, babies of either sex can be born on January 2nd, and both men and women can be "Queens" by birth. So, if you are a man, and the Queen happens to be your birthcard, then you would embody the qualities of the Queen, but in a male-oriented way. Perhaps you are an especially nurturing person or parent, or maybe you have talent in teaching or instructing others. Also, it's good to remember that there are some characteristics of royalty that seem to be universal. For instance, they both lead best by example.

If your reading contains multiple Queens, you will most likely enjoy a time of meeting with mature women in positions of power and authority.

♥ *Queen of Hearts* ♥

Mercury Mature and loving communication, sacrifices made for others, teaching by being a loving example, conversations about social etiquette and proper behavior. Organizing your "people" or entourage.

Venus Mother Mary, unconditional love in its highest form. The power of charm, goodwill, and self-sacrifice. Teaching in the home, blessed events, female children or grandchildren, organizing your family finances or home, the mother or grandmother.

Mars The power of charisma to draw energetic support (or a crowd). Energy and drive, blessed events, the father or grandfather, male children or grandchildren.

Jupiter Gifts, good will (shown and bestowed), friends are a blessing. Taking others on a trip, a romantic tour guide, visits to friends and family (or they may visit you), family fun and friendly company.

Saturn A hard working woman, a female boss, heading up your own company, teaching takes hard work, patience and expertise, the power at the top. The right people for the right job.

Uranus A sudden meeting, teaching is exciting and spontaneous, using the internet or computer for success. Psychic power, emotional charm, a sudden influx of social activity with you at the center.

Neptune A spiritual or metaphysical woman, spiritual sacrifice, Mother Theresa, Yemaya (Queen of the Sea), the Goddess, the Divine Feminine. Kindness, compassion, empathy, a gentlewoman, women of the sea, holy water, liquid blessings, mermaids, the shell collector, the Sailmaker.

Pluto Motherhood can deeply transform you, challenged to love unconditionally and make sacrifices for loved ones. Quiet power moves silently but in important and in-depth ways.

SUMMARY: The theme of the reading is about unconditional love. So, motherhood, teaching, nurturing family, caring for the next generation (or the previous one) are all likely to be themes now. You also may be called upon to teach someone the true meaning of friendship by your example. Lucky for you, the Queen of Hearts is the very picture of grace under fire.

BIRTH CARD: If the Queen ♥ is your Birth Card, you rule over the world of relationships. And your card is one that can juggle a lot of people at one time and keep all the balls in the air. But beware of trying to organize hearts the way you organize your home! People are not knick-knacks and you can't just move them about at will (they are also not interchangeable with one another!). You will have many opportunities to help families in need (even our own). Remember that your card represents the Goddess of Divine Love and act accordingly.

♣ *Queen of Clubs* ♣

Mercury Wise counsel given or recieved, the brilliant strategist. Diana, Goddess of the hunt. Mentoring others, the teacher, guru, advice columnist.

Venus An elegant speaker or writer, diplomacy, witty. An intelligent and charming conversationalist.

Mars Harnessing the passion of youth into worthy ideals. A passionate appeal, energetic ideas, an intense attraction or relationship.

Jupiter Writing or speaking about your travels, the seasoned travel guide, the world traveller, the global citizen.

Saturn Efforts to network, responsibilities with underlings, mentoring people at work, teaching others complex subject matter, patience, expertise.

Uranus Sudden communication from someone at the top, the principal of a school, the teacher gives a pop quiz, being tested. An impromptu (but valuable) lesson.

Neptune The spiritual novitiate, Mother Superior, the Goddess, the Divine Feminine. Leading the congregation, teaching by example. Spiritual ideals used to better the lives of others, writing meditations, telling angel stories. The voice raised in prayer, elevated words.

Pluto Your own depth and complexity transforms you, a deep or intense relationship with a mature woman. A powerful woman with something important to say. Reaching a large audience. Your teachings transform others.

SUMMARY: The theme of the reading is the power of the written or spoken word, especially when coming from the top. Your words carry great weight and authority and you can reach your audience with intelligence and conviction now. Expect to deal with (or become) a mature, experienced woman who mentors talent, nurtures the mind, and teaches the inexperienced.

BIRTH CARD: If the Queen ♣ is your Birth Card, you rule over the world of communication. And your card is one that can juggle a lot of conversations at one time and keep all the balls in the air. But beware of trying to organize your thoughts the way you organize your data! People do not want to talk to computers, they want live operators. You will have opportunities to teach others and many of your ideas can help people. Your influence is considerable without being overbearing, and a word from you in the right ear can change everything. Remember that your card represents the Goddess of Divine Wisdom and act accordingly.

◆ *Queen of Diamonds* ◆

Mercury The banker, organizing your finances, lecturing the class, mentoring youth, conversations about values.

Venus Aphrodite, the power to attract. The consumate hostess, an expensive affair, the upper crust, the Ice Queen. Women of influence, family business, mom sends a check (and her love).

Mars The consummate host, a passionate affair, dealing with men of influence, family business (working/dealing with male relatives), using your passion and drive to generate an income.

Jupiter A generous woman, a benefactress. The Principal or Headmistress, running the school, teaching something of value. Travelling First Class. Your expansive teachings and dependable methods win your students respect.

Saturn Working hard at networking, people come with responsibilities, friends at work, mixing business and pleasure, paying taxes, dealing with antiques or history, items that accrue in value over time.

Uranus A sudden meeting, surprise (or uninvited) guests, erratic, unpredictable people may pop up, or you may run into interesting and unique people. Handling the paparazzi, class differences (the rich really are different), women increase your business. Financial news is surprising.

Neptune Combining financial and spiritual values, backing what you believe in, charitable donations, fundraising. The benefactress or patron, helping those who can't help themselves. The Goddess, the Divine Feminine. Teaching by practicing what you preach.

Pluto A mature value system transforms you, an immature one can break you. Grabbing for money is like grasping at straws. Knowing what's important and what isn't, deciding what has true value to you, knowing what a thing is really worth.

SUMMARY: The theme of the reading is knowing your own true worth. Once you have defined your own sense of inner prosperity, you can then teach others to define theirs as well. This may also be a time of assisting others financially. Establishing a strong sense of core values will sustain and support your entire family. You can successfully organize financial details now. And you will finally be paid what you're worth.

BIRTH CARD: If the Queen ♦ is your Birth Card, you rule over the world of finance and resources. And your card is one that can juggle a lot of accounts at one time and keep all the balls in the air. But beware of trying to organize your values the way you organize your checkbook! Values like loyalty and respect cannot be bought, you'll need to earn them. You will have many opportunities to contribute to philanthropic causes and humanitarian efforts and to provide security for others. Remember that your card represents the Goddess of Divine Abundance and act accordingly.

♠ *Queen of Spades* ♠

Mercury A quick exchange of information, organizing one's thoughts, lots on the mind, teaching, training, mentoring, communicating, writing, dispensing sage advice.

Venus It's good to be the Queen! Working at home, organizing the home, guiding or mentoring family, resolving issues with one's mother (or daughter), a professional appearance.

Mars Controlling one's own passions, drives and ambitions, resolving anger or issues with one's mother (or son).

Jupiter Mastering both business and spiritual life, good fortune (as in "fortune favors the prepared"), progress in one's teaching or studies. Travelling with purpose, the experienced trail guide, the tracker.

Saturn Overcoming health or work obstacles thru self-control and mature effort, activities surrounding real estate or property.

Uranus A sudden revelation at work or on the job, learning or teaching metaphysical studies, a woman acting impulsively or spontaneously. Suddenly seeing yourself or your situation clearly, transforming yourself in surprising ways.

Neptune Mastery over your hopes and dreams, intuition, meaningful dreams full of depth, a powerful and talented psychic, the wise old gypsy woman, Romani. The Goddess, the Divine Feminine. Compassion in its highest form. Mary Magdalene.

Pluto The answer to your problem is to transform yourself (not others), learning about the nature of true power (and how to take yours back).

SUMMARY: The theme of the reading is selfless service to others, teaching, and leading others by your good example. You have an opportunity now to use your considerable power and influence to further the needs of others. And don't forget that helping others get what they want can bring good karma back around. This is a good time to organize your daily affairs and to fortify your health through better choices.

BIRTH CARD: If the Queen ♠ is your Birth Card, you rule over the work world. And your card is one that can juggle a lot of projects at one time and keep all the balls in the air. But beware of trying to organize your project teams the way you organize pieces on a chessboard! Although you will no doubt have many ideas for how to help employees and improve things on the job, the members of your team need to have some reason to buy into your plan. Health will also be a very important theme–both your own health as well as the health of others–and "nurturing" others may be quite literal. You may find charitable or philanthropic ways to provide food or shelter for others. Remember that your card represents the Goddess of Divine Purpose and act accordingly.

Kings

♥ ♣ ♦ ♠ ♥ ♣ ♦ ♠

The Kings (or Thirteens) represent maturity and masculinity. They are the model of fatherhood and protection, and embody the qualities of leadership and authority. They make excellent leaders. On an esoteric level, they represent the God and the Divine Masculine.

Kings are usually men, however they can also just represent those qualities generally associated with men, as either gender may encompass both male and female traits. In general though, the Kings usually represent fathers, mature men and/or men in authority. However, one exception to this general rule is if any of the King cards happens to be your personal Birth Card (and you can look up your Birth Card in the section entitled *Your Birth Card*).

Let's say, for example, that you were born on January 1st, of any year. That would make your birthcard the King of Spades. Obviously, babies of either sex can be born on January 1st, and both men and women can be "Kings" by birth. So, if you are a woman, and the King happens to be your birthcard, then you would embody the qualities of the King, but in a female-oriented way. Perhaps you are an especially protective person or parent, or maybe you have talent in heading up organizations or making executive decisions. Also, it's good to remember that there are some characteristics of royalty that seem to be universal. For instance, they both lead best by example.

If your reading contains multiple Kings you will likely have a time of meeting with mature men in positions of power and authority.

♥ *King of Hearts* ♥

Mercury Leading the conversation in a loving manner, speaking from the heart, successful speeches.

Venus Relationship success, leading your family or group, a solid emotional base. Warm family gatherings, the home is working well.

Mars An offer comes from a successful man. Channeling strong passions and drives into action for success. Leading the pack. The Alpha Dog.

Jupiter People power, your subjects adore you! Applause and well-wishers. Parties to celebrate you.

Saturn Being responsible for loved ones, maturity in love, becoming a father or authority figure. Head of the family. Firm but loving guidance.

Uranus A helping hand appears out of nowhere, a gesture of friendship or love takes you by surprise. People may think more of you than you realize.

Neptune Intuition used in a spiritual way, helping others is its own reward, charity begins at home.

Pluto Authority transforms you, controlling your emotions is the key to long-term success. Being a bully won't get you anywhere. Mature relationships=successful action. The God, the Divine Masculine.

SUMMARY: The theme of the reading is leading by using your people skills successfully. You have people power now! You may also be called upon to be a parent or to mentor others in some way, and fatherhood will also be an important theme. There is a solid emotional base that underlies and supports everything else in your life at this time. Your job now is to lead those you care for in a loving manner, as you fulfill your family duties and responsibilities.

BIRTH CARD: If the King ♥ is your Birth Card, you rule over the world of relationships. Because you were born to personally lead people, you must do so by example. Always treat others as you would want to be treated. This makes you a good role model for those who would follow you and it safeguards your personal reputation. Your impressive people skills will always be just as important to your overall success, as your natural charisma is. You are a person of strong emotion, and your passion to help others can be contagious. Your own personal relationship style–for good or ill–will be reflected in those who surround you.

♣ *King of Clubs* ♣

Mercury Leading the conversation by presenting the facts, discussing the data, getting ahead by having the right information. Signing important documents. Excellent oratory skills, making successful speeches, inspiring others with words. Mastery of the language. The Professor.

Venus Peace and quiet in the home, successful relationships with friends and family, teaching, writing home (or writing from home). Social charm and charisma.

Mars Successfully focusing your attention in order to achieve your ambitions, channeling your thoughts in one direction, using your own drive or passion for success, working with successful men, a successful debate or campaign.

Jupiter Interesting travel companions and guides, leading the tour, successful trips, teaching and learning, winning over students with expansive thoughts and ideas.

Saturn Mental work brings success, using what you know takes you to the top, leading with authority.

Uranus Helpful ideas appear out of the blue, brilliance, inspiration strikes. Getting your big plans off the ground, flying high.

Neptune Psychic information and imagination used successfully, creative work is inspired (and can inspire others). Talking about dreams (yours or anothers), and believing in them, can inspire you all to reach higher. Serving the community by manifesting your highest good.

Pluto Transformed by the power of the mind, a disciplined mind transforms you and brings success, formulating a long-range plan, in-depth and intense communication or writing. Challenged to think your ideas all the way through—from concept to completion. The God, the Divine Masculine.

SUMMARY: The theme of the reading is leading with strong communication or successful concepts. You'll know just what (and how much) to say now and will be able to use words to win others over. Some other options may include political rallies, leading a cause, or writing inspirational speeches. As your influence builds, you will gain support for your ideas. This comes through the expression of mature attitudes and well defined opinions and as the result of disciplined thought, where you think your ideas all the way through to completion. Your job now is to lead others with a strong mental outlook, and a finished, polished plan.

BIRTH CARD: If the King ♣ is your Birth Card, you rule over the world of communication. Because your words carry greater weight as a leader, you will be held accountable for fully developing your thoughts and speaking in a responsible manner. You must always safeguard your intellectual properties, and set a good example for those who would follow your ideas. Disciplining your mind, and developing wisdom, will always be just as important to your overall success as your impressive IQ is. Your own philosophies and ideas—both rational and irrational—will be reflected in those who surround you.

✦ *King of Diamonds* ✦

Mercury Leading the conversation based on costs, fiscal meetings and discussions, setting the budget, money-making ideas.

Venus Women-owned businesses, financial success in the arts, mansions and expensive homes, trust funds.

Mars Captains of industry, financial ambitions realized, the head of household, working with men of influence and power. Dad sends a check (and his approval).

Jupiter Successful business expansion, adding value, money to grow on, business capital. Traveling like royalty (1st class!), an expensive trip or vacation, interesting travel companions or guides, leading the tour. Winning others over with solid values, counting your blessings.

Saturn The money power you've earned now comes to you, leading your company to financial success, being true to your personal values, staying the course, investments rise, your stock has accrued in value over time. Fiscal responsibility. CFO.

Uranus Your stock rises, financial brilliance, a surprise loan or gift, marketing or notoriety that leads to financial rewards. Suddenly realizing your true worth, or knowing exactly what you value.

Neptune Financial intuition, or backing from someone at the top. A large endowment, charitable donations. Trickle down economics? If you want your company to have solid spiritual values, then you must live up to that image yourself. Either the spiritual leader or the blind leading the blind.

Pluto Challenged to live up to your own value system, setting an example then following it, seeing your own true worth transforms you. Releasing all hypocrisy creates in-depth change and true leadership. The God, the Divine Masculine.

SUMMARY: The theme of the reading is leading your business to financial success. This is the time to know exactly what the bottom line is, both financially and personally. A foundation built on solid values helps the entire structure stand taller and stronger and knowing your own worth is the prerequisite to real world success. Your job now is to lead your team to the finish line by making sure your balance sheet is in the black.

BIRTH CARD: If the King ♦ is your Birth Card, you rule over the world of finance and developing your resources will always be an important part of your life. And you will be held accountable for your department's success or, if you own your own business, for your own company's success. Your own personal value system will guide you in forming a solid foundation from which you can grow your business and expand your sphere of influence. Because part of your destiny is to help those you lead to achieve their own financial success, your own prosperity may be just as important as theirs is, and will be reflected in those who surround you. "The Buck Stops Here" is quite literally your motto.

♠ *King of Spades* ♠

Mercury Leading the conversation based on goals, discussions about health and wellbeing. A disciplined mind, words of wisdom heal now, saying what you know to be true based on life experience (as opposed to books). Decisions worthy of a ruler, occasions worthy of a King.

Venus Emotional self-control, successful home and family life, success with women and the arts, excellent health. The woman behind (or upon) the throne.

Mars It's good to be the King! Energetically achieving your goals, success with men and contests of strength, vibrant health. Passionately leading others, focused (or naked) drive and ambition.

Jupiter Being King of the Castle means taking on a leadership role, leading by example, mentoring, being a benevolent ruler (as opposed to a despot).

Saturn Using your expertise, sticking to your guns, "I know what I'm doing because I've been doing it long enough to know." Overcoming work or health obstacles by taking charge, taking full responsibility, "heavy the head that wears the crown," leading the next generation. CEO.

Uranus The early bird gets the worm. Success requires decisive action or a quick response, "just do it," a surprising offer of assistance or loyalty.

Neptune Intuitive success, hidden information benefits you, proprietary data, "for your eyes only," eye doctor, dreams of being at the top. Heading up a metaphysical or spiritual business. Caring for the rich and the poor equally.

Pluto Challenging yourself to produce your very best efforts for the good of all, achievement-oriented. Self-control allows you to achieve your goals and transform your life. The God, the Divine Masculine. Success allows you to take your power back and then to the next level where you can transform others. But using power the wrong way will sink you now. Ask yourself–like the Oracle in The Matrix Reloaded– *"What do all men with power want?...More Power."*

SUMMARY: The theme of the reading is leadership and a willingness to lead by example. This is the time to walk your talk. Your job is to lead by mirroring success. Others will follow your example, so make sure it's an exemplary one. Time to take charge, you're the "man with the plan" now, but make sure you would be capable of doing whatever it is you're asking others to do. Whether a Captain of Industry or the King of the Castle, you must put all who depend upon you first. The King is most definitely privileged, as he or she is the one in charge; but such privilege brings with it responsibilities. Survey all you own with pride, then thank those who helped you succeed. You can successfully achieve all you've worked for now.

BIRTH CARD: If the King ♠ is your Birth Card, you will rule at work, and developing your many and varied projects as well as employees will take center stage. Because you were born to lead in some area of business, you must always safeguard your reputation and set a good example for those who would follow you. Strengthening your physical health, and paying attention to the signals your body sends you will always be just as important to your overall success, as your sharp business acumen is. You are a person of action, but your actions may be curtailed if you neglect your health. Your own well being will be reflected in those who surround you.

The Ace of Spades
♥ ♣ ♦ ♠ ♥ ♣ ♦ ♠

An epic poem by Taryn DiGiacomo

Once there were four Queens and four Kings,
And four Jacks as well, just to liven things.
These royals did not actually have a kingdom,
But instead a deck contained them.
They were playing cards and very noble,
Their suits set in colors immobile.
The greatest of those cards, the noblest of them all,
Was the Ace of Spades, who above the rest stood tall.
Similar to that greatest of entertainers with one eye,
The Ace was unappreciated in his own time.
For Aces were once considered a lowly sort,
And dealings with them were little and short.
But let us continue with our story,
Which leads, ultimately, to one Ace's glory.

Now the King and Queen of Hearts were kind;
Never a dearer pair you'd find.
The Diamonds ruled as a royal pair,
That, save money, had no other care.
Not unlike the king of that blackbird rhyme
That sat in the counting-house all of the time.
The ruling Clubs were the scholarly ones,
Studying and reading books by the tons.
They liked to read many philosophies
Those of Plato, Heraclitus and Parmenides.
And lastly, the Spades King and Queen:
These royals believed in working and gleamed
With pride when they thought of what they'd done.
For their "kingdom" was surely a prize hard-won.
Ever-toiling day and night,
The Spades had made their suit bright.

All these cards thought they ruled fair and true;
Surely there was nothing they would do
If they had to change something about their land;

(well, they admitted they'd tune the royal band).
Yes the systems they had were all working fine,
Until the day when one brave card crossed the line.
It happened one evening at dinnertime,
When the King and Queen of Hearts were kind
Enough to invite the others to their palace
To consume a feast quite fit for their palates.
And while those worthy eight sat round the heart's table
Eating and drinking as much as they were able,
That was when the Ace of Spades, a most worthy of cards,
Was led into the dining hall escorted by guards.

"What is the meaning of this!?" The Diamonds King cried.
For of course every King and Queen alive
Knew that Aces were the "ones" of the deck,
And worth far less than the smallest peck
Of grain to the royal rulers dining there.
Surely an Ace to a King could not compare!
Said the King of Clubs, "Keep your talk fast and small,
In the name of that one who holds judgment over all."

"Hold! Let me Speak!" the brave Ace pressed,
"I come with a warning for you cards that seem the best."
"Harrumph," The King of Spades grumbled, considering;
"All right, we'll listen, but mind! Your time is dwindling."
The Ace drew himself up with dignity and strength.
And proceeded to tell of his warning at length.
"The other cards are planning to raise quite a din,
The way you've been ruling, to them is a sin!
If you want to prevent a major travesty,
Meaning no disrespect to your Majesties,
You're going to have to change some things.
Or deal with the horror tomorrow brings!
I who have come to warn you fully
Was chosen by the others, who recognize me
As no lowly Ace, but in fact
An equal member of our whole pack.
And perhaps their views changed because it was I, masters,
Who spoke to them of greener pastures."
The shocked Kings and Queens sat back at this last,

Thinking back onto the ways of their past,
And wondered if anything really needed fixing.
Hadn't they ruled as well as they'd been thinking?
And could the Ace actually be
As illuminated as he claimed they should see?

The Ace, encouraged by their silence went on:
"I know it's a difficult task to take upon
Yourselves, but you know that you must
If you want to be rulers good and just."

The King and Queen of Hearts thought back
On all the days they were mean to their Jack
And like so many others; those thoughts had been
Put aside until now, demanding to be seen.
The King and Queen of the noble Diamond suit
Thought back on each day they'd spent counting their loot.
To servants and the like they'd applied the lash
Preferring instead to count their cash.
The rulers of the Clubs were quite distraught
Upon realizing each thing they'd been taught
Was not that meaningful, compared with all
They'd lose if their people arranged their fall.
And those blue-blooded Spades, how they did weep!
When seeing just what their hard work had reaped.
Naught but sorrow for their subjects loyal,
All those years of strife and toil!
"Oh we've been such fools!" the Spades did cry,
"Our wondrous reign has been a lie!"
"We've been so blind," said the Diamond King,
"We've cared only for money; save that—not a thing!"
"I feel like a fool," cried the Hearts Queen in tears,
"We've only been selfish all these years."
"All that time and I was reading," lamented the Clubs King,
"Compared to ruling my kingdom, what can a book bring?"

"Your Majesties! Hear me!" said the Ace, "It is not too late
To save this deck from a deadly fate!
If you can mend your ways straight away,
Tomorrow will bring a brighter day.

I will speak now before our kingdom
And let them know of the changes you'll bring them."
And so the Royals agreed to mend their ways,
And to brighten up all future days,
And since they chose that wise and just path,
They were no longer the object of their subjects' wrath.
Instead things in the deck were soon happy as could be,
And Aces were realized as very worthy.
In fact, an award the Kings to the Ace gave;
A prized gift for one so valiant and brave.

The moral of this story is plain,
Hopefully I'm not saying this in vain.
Indeed bravery is always good.
If you have it, display it you should.
But don't think that data makes up one's whole life,
Or riches, or yourself alone, or hard work or strife.
Love should also be brought into it;
Don't live a life without kindness in it;
But instead include others around you
And you just might find this story to be true
And like the Royals always heed this advice:

Never underestimate the power of just being nice!

Recommended Reading

♥ ♣ ♦ ♠ ♥ ♣ ♦ ♠

This list of resources is in no way intended to be a complete reference. They are simply books I found personally useful when I began to research the card system of divination. These books are listed in order from oldest to newest. Some may be quite rare, out of print, or hard to find at this point, but might still be obtainable through used book stores, ebay, or other online sources. Some are easier to read and understand than others. But in my opinion (when you can find them), all are worth the effort.

The Mystic Test Book, by Olney H. Richmond, 1893,
The Temple Publishing Company, Chicago, IL

Symbolism, by Milton Alberto Pottenger, 1905, Symbol Publishing Company, Sacramento, CA

Astrology and the Cards, by E.H. Bailey, original date 1931, (reprinted by Astro-Cards Enterprises, Scottsdale, AZ)

Sacred Symbols of the Ancients, by Florence Evylinn Campbell and Edith L. Randall, 1947, DeVorss & Co, Marina del Rey, CA (out of print)

What's Your Card? by Arne Lein, 1978, Meta-Card, Santa Monica, CA, (out of print and hard to find)

Spreads Set & Card Titles, by Iain McLaren-Owens, 1994, Astro-Cards Enterprises, Scottsdale, AZ

Destiny Cards, and *Love Cards,* both by Robert Lee Camp, 1997, 1998, Sourcebooks, Naperville, IL

The Playing Card Oracles, by Ana Cortez, 2002, Two Sisters Press, Denver, CO

The God Clock, by Thomas Morrell, 2015, Davenport, IA

Card Reading Worksheet

(daily, weekly, monthly, solar return, etc.)

Name: _____   Card _____

Planetary Period	Start date	Cards	Notes
☿ Mercury			
♀ Venus			
♂ Mars			
♃ Jupiter			
♄ Saturn			
♅ Uranus			
♆ Nepune			
♇ Pluto			
Summary			

Card Decks Online
♥ ♣ ♦ ♠ ♥ ♣ ♦ ♠

If you prefer to purchase your cards online, there are certainly dozens of websites selling card decks from which to choose—some standard, some not. Here are just a few of the more impressive ones. They are listed in alphabetical order.

Art of Play: www.artofplay.com. This is a delightful site with artistic and unusual card decks. They have a Halloween deck called "Sleepy Hollow" with Pumpkin Head Jokers!

Bicycle® Brand Playing Cards: www.bicyclecards.com. An oldie but goodie, has been around for about 130 years. Gotta love the classics.

The House of Cards: www.thehouseofcards.com. I found a "Bacon" deck of cards here, with pigs as the court cards and sausages as pips... because....welll...umm...who doesn't love bacon? They also carry standard decks and art decks.

MPC: www.makeplayingcards.com. This site allows you to design your own original and one-of-a-kind decks of cards right online.

Piatnik: www.piatnikcardgames.co.uk. Unusual Viennese playing cards and older European designs. They also have a US website: **www. piatnik.us.**

ASSAltenburger: www.spielkartenladen.de; www.spielkartenfabrik. de; www.cartamundi.com. 'Spielkarten' means 'playing cards' in German. Here you will find some truly beautiful German card decks, along with French, Swiss and other European decks. The town of Altenburg in Germany is known as "the town of SKAT" because the game was invented there. And their card factory has been producing cards for hundreds of years. My grandmother would have loved this!

The United States Playing Card Company. www.usplayingcard.com. Carries all of my old faves, such as the Bicycle®, Tally-Ho®, Hoyle®, "Bee"® and the Aviator® brand playing cards. They also carry many new and colorful specialty decks. Check them out!

The World of Playing Cards: wopc.co.uk. Carries absolutely gorgeous, old world, playing cards. Very artistic site, includes cards from nearly every country.

Well, unfortunately, Olney H. Richmond, Florence Campbell, Edith Randall and Arne Lein are now deceased (although, if you are a medium, go for it). I don't claim to know every good reader of course; but surely there are other living, breathing sages out there who can help you in your quest for more information on the cards.

Here, I offer a few resources for your consideration:

Deane Driscoll: Our Cosmic Dance, Telephone: (828) 357-5411; email: **deane@ourcosmicdance.com. www.ourcosmicdance.com.** I am a professional astrologer, teacher and writer and hold elder clergy credentials as Lady Deane with CoG (Covenant of the Goddess). I offer readings, custom meditations and classes, and teach the card reading method my grandmother used. See the Cartomancy section of my website for more information, or to obtain the digital version of this manual.

Iain McLaren-Owens: Astro-Cards Enterprises, P.O. Box 12481 Scottsdale, AZ 85267; Telephone: (480) 421-0142; email: astro-cards@usa.net. Iain has an absolutely encyclopedic knowledge on the cards system. He has done some truly original research and is a treasure trove of information. He offers readings, classes and many books. Call or email him for his current list of available resources.

Thomas Morrell: 5500 North St, Bettendorf, IA 52722; Telephone: (563) 449-6110; thegodclock@gmail.com; **magiccrown.tripod.com.** Thomas is the creator of the **Ancient Book of Time System of Symbolic Astrology,** a unique method of card reading. He offers readings and books on cartomancy. Call or email him for his current list of available resources.

Other practicing teachers and readers of the cards may be found through the International Association of Cardology (IAC): **www.cardology.org.**

Deane Driscoll is a professional astrologer, card reader, teacher and writer with over 33 years of experience. In addition, Deane holds elder clergy credentials as **Lady Deane** with **CoG** (Covenant of the Goddess). She offers natal chart readings as well as classes in astrology, card reading, and other metaphysical topics.

Deane originally learned Cartomancy (the art of reading using an ordinary deck of playing cards) from her grandmother, when she was very young. And she learned about the planets, the stars, and the night sky while sailing with her father and her brother, Don, on Long Island. She shares the secrets her family taught her in "The Mystical Card Reading Handbook."

Deane also designs and records custom meditations to help individuals focus on their personal goals. And she writes timely articles detailing the cosmic dance going on just over our heads called "The New Moon Ballroom."

The heavens are perpetually in motion. Don't miss out on the dance! Sign up for Deane's free newsletter by visiting her website at **ourcosmicdance.com**

Deane and Dad

tiny baby psychic

Other books you might enjoy...

Past Lives, Future Choices
by Maritha Pottenger

Reincarnation helps to explain many phobias, dysfunctional family patterns, eating disorders, chronic pain, and other long-term problems. Using the ancient art of astrology, the reader can get instant access to possible past lives. Important, repetitive issues can be addressed - and solved! By looking backward, people are able to move forward to fulfillment.

The Palmistry Textbook
by Peter Burns

Whether you are an interested beginner or an experienced advisor in the helping-healing professions, you'll find this book to be a fascinating read, as well as a useful tool for personality and psychological insight. Over 80 cleanly drawn illustrations and clearly written text make this a complete step-by-step guide to hand analysis.

In this book you will learn to understand that the lines in your hands can and do change, just as we can change our lives! With hand analysis, we can identify the source of our difficulties, often before they manifest, and then adapt in ways that lead toward a more fulfilling future.

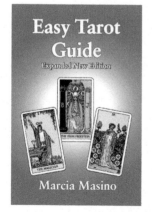

Easy Tarot Guide by Marcia Masino

This popular and best-selling Tarot book is the new Expanded Edition! Marcia Masino has substantially added to her valuable question and answer section from her vast experience as a Tarot advisor and instructor. Additionally, Marcia presents an entirely new and innovative chapter that combines meditation and yoga with Tarot. Marcia defines each card and its corresponding posture for a particular power in invoking and evoking archetypal energy to awaken soul purpose and gifts of the spirit. Each posture is carefully described in basic, advanced and simplified versions.

Books available through astrocom.com

CPSIA information can be obtained
at www.ICGtesting.com
Printed in the USA
LVOW02s2055190617
538610LV00018B/650/P